Christmas in Silverwood

T0170782

Other books by Dorothy Dreyer

Black Mariah series

Black Mariah: Hanau, Germany

Curse of the Phoenix series

Phoenix Descending

Paragon Rising

Empire of the Lotus Series

Crimson Mage

Copper Mage

Golden Mage

Emerald Mage

Sapphire Mage

Amethyst Mage

Diamon Mage

Awards

2018 New Apple Award for Outstanding Young Adult Fantasy

Christmas in Silverwood

DOROTHY DREYER

USA TODAY BESTSELLING AUTHOR

Christmas in Silverwood

This is a work of fiction. Names, characters, places, and incidents either are the product of the author's imagination or are used fictitiously.
Any resemblance to actual persons, living or dead, or locales is entirely coincidental.

Cover design by Michael J. Canales
www.MJCImageworks.com
and
Scotty Roberts
www.ScottAlanRoberts.com

ISBN: 978-1-64548-053-2

Published by Rosewind Romance
An imprint of Vesuvian Books
www.RosewindRomance.com

Printed in the United States

10 9 8 7 6 5 4 3 2 1

For Mom

Chapter One

H olly St. Ives clicked the button on the steering wheel that controlled the radio. The cheery melody of *Jingle Bell Rock* came to a stop. It wasn't just that she'd had enough of Christmas music, but she also needed to concentrate on the road. The snow was coming down hard, and she wasn't completely confident in the reliability of her snow tires. She squinted and ducked her head, as if the movement would help her to better see the sign up ahead.

Silverwood. Silverwood. She hoped she was going in the right direction. If only her navigation system hadn't been on the fritz, she might have a chance at reaching her destination before nightfall. She convinced herself she would recognize the area once she got nearer, but the truth was she hadn't been in Silverwood since she was a teenager. She resorted to following an app on her phone, but there was hardly any service this high in the mountains. *Or this far from civilization*, she thought to herself.

Her ringtone suddenly erupted from her phone, making her jump in her seat. She shook her head as she clicked the steering wheel's control button to answer the call.

She swallowed before she spoke. "Holly St. Ives."

"Hey, Holly-bear." Kim always sounded like she was whining. For the first couple years of their friendship, this annoyed the heck out of Holly. But now she'd gotten used to it. "How's the trip going?"

"Long. These mountain roads are never-ending."

"I know you probably hate that, but honestly I wish I could have left the city with you for a getaway. The construction outside the building is driving me batty. Don't they take a break for the holidays?"

"Not when they're getting time and a half. I guess everyone's got bills to pay." Which is exactly why Holly had left the city in the first place. She just couldn't afford her cushy New York apartment anymore. Things had been great when her paintings had graced the walls of every gallery exhibit in the city. But after a couple stellar years of hitting the big time, Holly found herself in a rut. Long gone was her joy and inspiration in the one thing she had been truly passionate about. Now it seemed as if being in the business was all about the publicity and the money. And that kind of pressure sucked all the delight out of Holly's creativity. Not to mention, her art simply wasn't selling recently. Living as a starving artist just wasn't cutting it.

"Did you call just to check up on me, Kim? Or was there something else you wanted to talk to me about?" Secretly, Holly had been hoping one of the galleries had been trying to reach her. Maybe instead of contacting her via email, her agent had showed up at her apartment building to deliver the great news in person. A last glimmer of hope to have her racing back to finish her dream.

"Well, there was another reason, but I don't think you're

going to like it."

Holly grimaced, preparing herself. "Just spill it."

"Grayson dropped off a box of your stuff."

For a moment, Holly was quiet, trying to process the fact that her ex had come by her apartment. The muscles in her neck tensed, and she pressed her lips into a straight line. "Grayson was there? Did you talk to him?"

"Yeah. I caught him standing in front of your door ringing your bell with a big cardboard box in his arms. So me, being the big-hearted neighbor I am, I told him you were out of town and took the box for you."

"But you didn't tell him specifically where I was going, did you?"

"No, of course not. He didn't call you to tell you he was coming by?"

Holly sighed. "I stopped answering his calls after the breakup. And eventually he stopped calling. I'm surprised he came by."

"So, what do you want me to do with the box?"

Holly worried her lip for a second. "It's probably all junk. You can get rid of it."

"Don't you want to check what's in the box first? There might be something sentimental or … valuable in it."

A laugh escaped Holly's lips. "Tell you what: you see something you like, you can have it. I really don't want to have anything that reminds me of that dead-end relationship. I mean, he's the one who stopped caring to ask how my day was or treating me like—you know what? I don't want to think about it. You're welcome to anything in there. Merry Christmas."

"Wow. Thanks, Holly."

"Don't mention it."

"Well, I better let you go." There was Kim's whiny voice again. "Don't want to distract you while you're driving. You might end up running over Big Foot or something."

Holly smirked. "Bye, Kim."

As she clicked on the END CALL button, she noticed a sign up ahead where there was a fork in the road. Snow clung to the sign, making it impossible to read. For a split second, she considered stopping and getting out to brush the snow off the sign. But that split second came and went. It was way too cold out to get out of the car. Judging from the look of the two roads, Holly decided to go right instead of left. It wasn't until she was a few miles down her chosen path that she found the road had narrowed to half its size, and the mass of trees flanking her journey grew thicker and thicker. In her head, she fought with herself. Half of her wanted to turn around and take the other road, but the other half of her told her to stick to her decision and follow her first instinct.

She rapped on her navigation device with her knuckles, hoping it would somehow come back to life. But she had no such luck. Her fingers tightened on the steering wheel as she took a tight curve. Up ahead, a big truck blocked her side of the road. The open bed of the truck was filled with Christmas trees. She slowed down and stretched her neck out, checking the road ahead. No one was coming from the opposite direction, so Holly proceeded to steer around the truck.

Something small and fuzzy suddenly zipped across the road in front of her car. Just as she instinctively let her foot off the gas pedal, something bigger and fuzzier bound across the road. With a gasp, Holly slammed on the brakes. Her car swerved on the snowy road. She jerked in her seat as the car dipped slightly in the ditch on the opposite side. Her life seemed to flash before her eyes at the sight of the tree her car was barreling toward, until she pulled the handbrake with a scream. She jolted forward against her seatbelt as the car came to a stop.

Frazzled, she fought to catch her breath. She felt as if her heart was in her throat, and she had to swallow hard to get it to go back to where it belonged. Once she got her wits about her, she unbuckled her seatbelt and threw her car door open. Her foot almost slipped out from under her as she stepped out into the snow. She made a mental note to wear her other pair of boots while up in the mountains. The ones with more traction to keep from slipping. She winced as the cold mountain air slapped her in the face. Holding on to the car, she made her way to the hood to check if there was any damage. The car was intact, and luckily, the roadside ditch wasn't deep enough for her to get stuck in.

At the sound of a bark, she jumped in her skin and turned to find the offender. She could have sworn the large, black and white dog staring at her was a wolf. Its tongue hung out as it panted. She wasn't sure what to do. The dog sat its butt down in the snow and lifted a paw at her, then jumped up and raced back across the road. Her gaze followed its course and found it approaching a tall, fit man lugging a medium-sized, chopped tree toward his truck bed. When the dog barked at the man, he straightened, noticing Holly and her car. Dropping the tree, the man walked toward her with purpose in his strides. He straightened his thick plaid coat and adjusted the wool bomber hat on his head. The dog barked again and rushed back to Holly.

"You all right?" the man asked. His voice was low and soothing.

"Is this your dog?" She hadn't meant to sound so unpleasant, but she was still shaken up from almost plowing her car into a tree. She was surprised she could hear her own voice above the hammering in her chest.

The dog waltzed up to her and tucked its head under Holly's hand before sitting in the snow again and panting at her. Was it actually smiling?

"You weren't hurt, were you?" the man asked, inspecting the position of the car.

"Well, your mutt almost got me killed."

The man narrowed his eyes. "Mutt? Cupid is a pure-bred Alaskan Malamute."

Cupid rolled over in the snow with its tongue sticking out. When it got back up on its paws, it shook to get the snow off its fur.

Holly flinched as bits of snow sprayed up onto her coat. "Oh, excuse me! Maybe you should teach your pure-bred not to chase squirrels across the road. What's he got against squirrels anyway? You'd think a dog named Cupid would have a heart for the poor creatures. What kind of saint is that?"

Cupid proceeded to sit in the snow again, raising its paw. Did the dog want to shake hands or something? She could have sworn it winked at her.

The man let out a small laugh.

"What's so funny?" Holly asked.

"First of all, I think Cupid's trying to offer his apologies. Secondly, I think you're thinking of the mythological god of love and attraction. There is no Saint Cupid. And third, he was actually named after the reindeer. You know, from the Rudolph song?"

Holly scoffed and shrugged.

The man rubbed at his bearded jaw. She'd been too worked up to notice, but now he'd drawn attention to his face. Underneath his wool bomber hat, the man actually had attractive features. Strong cheekbones, square jaw, and blue eyes that made her think of summer—wait, what was she doing?

"Whatever," was all she could think of to say as she fought off a blush. "Just get your dog out of the road."

"Look, sorry for the trouble. Do you need any help with your car? I've got some tow straps in the truck if you need help getting out of that snowbank."

Holly pursed her lips. "No, thanks. I can manage." She turned to head back to her car but then stopped suddenly. Letting out a frustrated breath, she swung back around to face him. "Can you tell me if this road leads to Silverwood?"

"Oh, you're headed to Silverwood?"

Holly narrowed her eyes at him. "Yeah."

The man smiled. "Yep, it sure does. Just keep following the road about twenty miles down and you'll see the sign."

Holly nodded her head once. "Thank you."

"The name's Nick, by the way." He said when she was almost at her car door.

She lifted her hand but didn't look back at him. She wasn't

sure why she was being so impolite to this handsome stranger. At the sound of a bark, she flinched, but refused to turn around. Was she crazy to think the dog was barking goodbye to her, wishing her a pleasant journey? Yeah, that was crazy.

Once she was in her car, she closed the door and turned the ignition key. After shifting into reverse, she pushed on the gas, but the car wouldn't budge. The engine simply revved without the car going anywhere.

"No, no, no." She didn't really want to have to ask Nick for help. She'd already felt like she made a fool of herself by being so rude to him. Glancing down, she realized she'd forgotten to disengage the handbrake.

Letting out a sigh of relief, she sheepishly glanced in her rearview mirror at Nick to see if he noticed. Nick stood where he had been, smirking with his hands in his coat pockets.

Cheeks burning, she expelled a huff of exasperation and drove off.

Once she was safely down the road, she let her shoulders sag and her head fall back against the headrest. Checking her rearview mirror, she caught Nick patting Cupid on the head before heading back to his truck. She shook her head, finding the encounter incredulous. Still, the man had been polite and didn't fight back with her, even though she knew she was the one being inexplicably rude. No, Nick had been a gentleman.

Nick, she thought. *That's a nice name.*

Chapter Two

The flurries seemed to dwindle, leaving a stray flake or two landing on Holly's windshield. Flanked by rows of snow-topped evergreens, the road widened a bit more, giving Holly a sense of reprieve. The sign up ahead filled her with relief, and she loosened her grip on the steering wheel a bit.

Welcome to Silverwood.

She'd made it.

The sky began to clear to a crystal blue, serving as a gorgeous backdrop to the distant housetops nestled in the cozy, mountainside, forest town. It wasn't until she got closer to the quaint village that she began to recognize some of the buildings and landmarks from the time she spent in Silverwood as a kid. Something bloomed inside her heart, something she hadn't felt in years.

It all came rushing back to her. She knew exactly which road to take to get to her destination. An invigorating feeling filled her as she took the familiar turns up the mountain road. It was as if she was a kid again, journeying up to her family's mountain cabin to tuck away for the holidays. Except now, she was in the driver's seat.

There were more houses now than she remembered, but the landscape mostly looked the same. Gorgeous, just like the picture she had in her mind. It was so serene here, she almost felt as if it wasn't real.

Her heart sped up as the cabin came into view. The charming, one-story home was picturesque, surrounded by pure white snow behind a picket fence. She pulled into the driveway, everything growing quiet as she turned off the car's engine. Holly took a moment, sitting in the parked car, gazing at the place that held so many treasured family memories. She hadn't stepped foot in the place since she was seventeen, and she'd never dreamed she would ever come here without her parents. It was bittersweet. She took in a slow breath and exhaled, feeling a tug at her heart.

"Yoohoo!"

Holly was snapped out of her trance by an older, robust woman in a light brown winter coat approaching her car.

"Holly, is that you?"

Unbuckling her seatbelt, Holly smiled at the woman through the window. The moment she stepped out of the car, she was enveloped in the woman's arms. She almost sneezed when the faux fur from the woman's coat tickled her nose. She patted the woman on the back, hoping she would let her go soon so she could breathe.

"My goodness it's been years." The woman stepped back and looked Holly up and down with a sentimental smile. "You're all grown up."

"Mrs. Miranelli. It's good to see you."

Mrs. Miranelli's smile faded, and she grasped Holly's hands in hers. "Oh, my dear. I was so sorry about your father's passing. Jake was always very kind."

Holly gave her a nod. "Thank you for saying that."

In the two years since her father's death, Holly had learned that it was best to simply thank those who offered their condolences. It kept her from digging too deeply into her sorrow and becoming a sobbing pile of mush.

"Where is Vivian?" Mrs. Miranelli asked.

"Oh, she moved back to the Philippines to stay with my aunt."

Mrs. Miranelli creased her brow. "So you've been living on your own in the states without family?"

Holly smiled at her and gave her a wink. "Yeah. I'm a big girl now."

"I can see that, dear. But are you spending the holidays by yourself?"

"Yes."

"Pretty young woman like you doesn't have a boyfriend to celebrate Christmas with?"

Holly could feel her face falling.

"Oh!" Mrs. Miranelli leaned closer. "I'm sorry for prying."

"It's okay." Holly waved a hand at her. "No, I'm single. And I'm fine."

The thought of her ex made her stomach churn a bit. She let out a breath and told herself to push thoughts of Grayson away.

"Well, that's all right." Mrs. Miranelli placed her hands on her hips. "You thinking of staying in Silverwood for good? You already have a great place to live."

"Oh, I don't know. I'm sort of between career moves, I guess you could call it. I'm taking the holidays to figure out what my next step is. Like a sabbatical. I'm not sure how long I'm staying, and I might sell the cabin."

"What? No!" Mrs. Miranelli looked flushed. "I mean, far be it from me to tell you what to do, but this cabin is a gem. Plus think of all the memories you had here. Those are irreplaceable. And Silverwood—well there's no better place to live."

Holly wondered if Mrs. Miranelli had ever lived anywhere else to speak with such authority. "I'll think about it, thanks. I should go in and get settled, though. I've still got some things to do."

"Oh, yes, of course."

Something in the corner of Holly's vision caught her eye. "Oh. What, uh, happened to the mailbox?"

The plain mailbox that stood near the front of the property was hanging crooked, propped up by a plank of wood.

"We had a bad storm blow through here last year. Took down some trees and broke our fence. Looks like it got your mailbox as well."

"Looks like someone tried to prop it up, though."

"Might have been the mailman. You know, in Silverwood, everyone is always looking out for each other."

"That's nice." Holly told herself to put fixing the mailbox on her list of things to do.

Mrs. Miranelli patted Holly on the shoulder. "Okay, dear. Now if you need anything, just let me know. The town's grown a bit since you've been gone. There's a bigger grocery store, which I'm sure you're going to want to get to. It's right next to that art school. You remember the one?"

"Yeah, sure. My parents let me do a couple classes there when

I was a kid. I know now that it was just so they could get their Christmas shopping done without me, but I, uh, remember those classes fondly."

"Oh, then you should definitely visit Mrs. Weedleman."

Holly felt her face light up. "Mrs. Weedleman still teaches there?"

"Well, not for long. She's going into retirement soon, I believe."

"Yeah, I'll have to pay her a visit. It'll be nice."

"You do that." Mrs. Miranelli looked over her shoulder at her house down the road a bit and across the street. "Okay, dear, have fun settling in. Hop on over if you need anything. I'll see you around."

"Thanks, Mrs. Miranelli. I appreciate it."

Holly turned to the cabin and walked up the front step, telling herself she would deal with her luggage later. A strange chill came over her as she unlocked the front door. Something about the click that sounded as she turned the key woke a dormant melancholy in her heart. This would be the first time she would stay in the cabin without hearing her father's soothing bass voice singing Christmas carols. The first time she would spend time in the family getaway without the people that made it feel like home.

She pushed the door open and switched on the light, thankful the electricity had been turned on like she had requested. She stood in the main room looking around. Everything was in place exactly where she'd remembered them. Memories of Christmases past played out in her mind, with the ghost of her father dominating every scene. Holly let out a shuddered breath and traveled farther into the room.

She took her boots off, remembering how her mother never let anyone walk around inside with shoes on. That was probably part of the reason the hardwood floors still looked like new. She set them down on the hearth of the fireplace. She made a note to get a fire started after she went through the house. She realized how different the fireplace looked without Christmas stockings hung or one of her mom's beautiful Christmas centerpieces adorning the mantle.

The old couch in the living area was covered with a large white sheet. She braced herself as she removed it, ready for flying dust to attack her. She wrapped the sheet up as she fought off a dust-induced cough. The blue tone of the couch fabric was more faded than she recalled, and it would probably benefit from a blast of fresh air. Though she knew it would be cold, she opened a few windows to freshen the place up.

On her way around the house to slide open some windows, the bare cupboards and empty refrigerator in the kitchen reminded her she'd need to pick up some groceries and other supplies. Heading toward the back of the house, she decided to claim the bigger bedroom—the one that used to be her parents'—rather than the small bedroom with the twin-sized bed she had as a kid. She hoped the sheets in the linen closet were fresh enough, otherwise she'd have to pop them in the washer and dryer before bedtime.

The last part of the house she checked was the garage. As soon as she opened the door that connected the main part of the house to the garage, her eyes widened at the sight of the enormous tarp-covered object standing in place of a car. More memories flooded back to her, this time of all the Christmas holidays her father spent utilizing his carpentry skills.

She approached the tarp with a smile on her face. Standing on her tiptoes, she grabbed a section of the tarp. The plastic material crackled as she pulled it off, blatant evidence that it hadn't been touched in a long time. As the flying sawdust and debris cleared, Holly gazed in wonder at the hand-crafted sleigh. It was one of her father's finest works. It was beautiful, with its perfectly sanded curves and polished rails. She could picture the concentration on her father's face when he'd meticulously weather-proofed it. He was a perfectionist when it came to the sleigh, paying attention to every detail. There was a plump, red cushion on the front bench, big enough to fit two adults. Holly remembered sitting on the bench with her father as he pretended to drive it through the snow—though it had never left the garage. The back compartment was just the right size to carry sacksful of gifts for the whole town. At least, that was how Holly had always imagined it: as the perfect sleigh for Santa. She ran her hand along the wood, wondering what had inspired her father to build it. Of course, spending the holidays in a winter wonderland might have had something to do with it. She felt it a shame that he'd never taken it out for a test run. She knew there were stables not too far away that probably would have been happy to help them out with horses to rein. Instead, the sleigh sat in the cabin's garage for years, untouched.

A cool breeze brushed by her, making the hairs on her skin rise. She rubbed at her arms, remembering she'd left a good number of windows open in the house. Grabbing a few logs of wood from the stack in the garage, she headed back inside to warm the place up again.

Once all the windows were properly shut, Holly knelt before the fireplace, making sure the flue was open so she could start a fire. Stacking the wood from the hearth to the metal rack in the fireplace, she was struck with the memory of her father teaching her how to light a fire. He always did the heavy lifting, but he did let her use the fireplace lighter on the fire-starting cubes. The kindling grew bright with flames, and Holly stood back to admire her work. The picture frame on the mantle caught her eye. She reached out and took it down to inspect more closely, running her finger over the images of her parents. It was taken before Holly was born, and her parents looked like teenagers in the shot.

She missed them so much.

After bringing in her suitcases, she pulled out her phone and pressed the contact button for her mother. She'd promised she would call as soon as she got in, and she didn't want to worry her.

"Holly?"

Holly smiled at the sound of her mom's voice. "Hi, Mom. I'm in the cabin."

"Oh, good. You made it. I was worried about the snowy roads. You know how much driving in the snow freaks me out."

Holly let out a small laugh.

"How's the cabin?" her mom asked.

"It, uh, looks the same. Just with added dust."

"I'm sorry I can't fly in to spend Christmas with you, honey. But Auntie Lita needs me."

"No, I understand." Holly plopped down on the couch, pulling a throw pillow onto her lap. "I don't really like to celebrate

Christmas anyway."

"What? How can you say that? You used to love Christmas."

"Back when I was a kid."

"No, I remember even a few years ago, you'd get excited when the holidays came. We came to see you in New York, remember?"

"Yeah. But … that was before dad passed away. Things seem a lot bleaker now."

A silence fell between them for a moment. Holly really didn't want to upset her mother, and she didn't want the conversation to be a downer.

"Guess what's still sitting in the garage," Holly said.

"What could be—No. Wow, I'd forgotten about that sled."

Holly laughed again. "It's a sleigh, Mom."

"Sleigh, right. So, it's still standing?"

"Sleeping in a blanket of dust is more like it. What did he ever mean to do with that thing?"

"Oh, you know. It was just one of his creative projects. You inherited your penchant for art from him, you know. It was probably for one of the town's Christmas festivals. Maybe you could donate it."

"Yeah, sure." Holly could feel the flames of the fire heating the room. She tucked her hair behind her ear. "I'll ask around and find out who's in charge."

"Okay, honey. I need to go. But I'll call you on Christmas, okay?"

"Okay, Mom. Take care. Talk to you soon."

"Glad you got back to Silverwood safely. Miss you, baby!"

"Love you, Mom."

As she hung up, her stomach let out a grumble. She needed to figure out her food situation, and fast. She decided to shower and change, giving the fire a chance to die down before she headed into town. She felt the need to stretch her legs after all that driving, so a nice walk through the town square and finding a nice place to eat was the very thing she needed.

Chapter Three

Holly pressed the mail app on her phone. It was mostly out of habit, having spent the last several months waiting for a gallery to accept her work. But it was also out of desperation, wanting to hear good news from her agent. She needed to get out of this rut, and she knew if a gallery would just give her a chance, she could get a second wind and rise above this unfortunate bump in her career.

The only thing she found in her inbox was spam.

Merry Christmas to you, too, Nigerian prince.

Just as she was closing the mail app, she received an incoming call. Her finger was quicker than her eye, and as soon as she accepted the call, she realized too late that it was Grayson. She stared at the screen, hearing his voice floating out from her device as she decided whether or not to simply hang up.

"Holly? Holly, please."

With a scowl, she held the phone to her ear. "What?" she asked through gritted teeth.

He was quiet for a moment. "Don't hang up, okay? I, uh, wanted to talk to you."

"Why?" She released the fist she was making when her nails pierced the skin of her palm. "I didn't think we had anything more to discuss. The last thing you said to me was you were glad things were over because there was some 'hot babe'—your words, not mine—who was dying to get with you."

Grayson scoffed. "Those were just words of anger. Heat of the moment type of thing, Holly. I didn't mean them."

"There's a picture on Instagram that says differently."

"So, you're still checking my Instagram?"

She could practically feel him smirking his stupid, cocky smirk. "Not anymore."

"Come on, Holly. Why don't we discuss this in person? You, me, a couple of mojitos …"

"No, Grayson. It's over. Besides, I'm not in—" She cut herself off, not wanting him to know she'd left town. The last thing she needed was him following her to Silverwood to try to get back together. That ship had sailed. "I'm busy. You know, the holiday season and all?"

"The holiday season? You? Since when do you care about Christmas?"

She used to. Before it became all about making sales and keeping her name in the papers.

"There are a lot of things about me you never bothered to learn, Grayson." Just saying his name was making her stomach churn. "The only thing you cared about was my status in high society. And then one bump in the road and you suddenly had no time for me anymore."

He scoffed. "But it wasn't just one bump in the road. Was it,

Holly? How many years has it been since you've sold even a single piece of art?"

Holly could feel the heat rising in her neck. "What does that even have to do with our relationship? Couples are supposed to stick together during highs and lows. Be there for each other. I went to every work event you invited me to and listened to hours of you and your colleagues drone on about fiscal crap. It wasn't ideal but I was there for you. But you stopped showing up to my showings. And then you stopped showing up, period. Where was the support? You know what? It doesn't matter anymore. I ended this months ago, and it's going to stay ended."

"Wait. No. Holly, don't say that. Listen, why don't I come over to your place and we can talk this over, face-to-face?"

"No, I—"

"Yes. Yes. It'll be good. I've got a bottle of wine. I'm wearing your favorite cologne. I'm hanging up, and I'll be right over."

The line went silent, and Holly stared at her phone. She let out the smallest of laughs. "Good luck with that."

She immediately went into his contact information and blocked him. There was nothing more to say, and she didn't need that negativity in her life anymore. She then went through all forms of social media she knew of and blocked him there as well. With a cringe, she tucked her phone away, knowing she'd be hearing from Kim about Grayson's attempts to find her. She just hoped Kim would keep her word about not revealing her whereabouts.

Zipping up her coat, she took a deep breath, ready to drive into town. On the dining room table, her camera stared back at her. She really wasn't in the mood to be creative and brilliant at the moment, but she knew inspiration could strike when least expected. Besides, wouldn't it be a kick in Grayson's backside if she got her inspiration back and created a masterpiece? He expected her to remain a failure, and she wasn't about to let him win. It wasn't the best reason to get back in the game, but it was a push, and she was going to use whatever she could to get back on track.

With a frustrated sigh, she grabbed the camera and hung the strap around her neck. *Hello, old friend. Ready to find a muse?*

Her mind wouldn't stop replaying the conversation with Grayson while she drove. She kept shaking her head and telling herself to think about something else, but it was no use. It wasn't until she came upon a truck blocking her side of the road that she finally turned off Grayson's voice in her head.

"Are you kidding me?"

She slowed down, checking left and right as she reduced her speed to walking pace. She didn't want another near collision with that crazy dog. Okay, he was cute, and it was actually funny how he kept raising his paw for her and rolled over in the snow. But she was never going to let Nick know she thought that. As she made her way around the truck, she stretched out her neck to see if she could catch a glimpse of Nick delivering a tree or whatever he was doing. She wasn't sure why he had to take up half the road as if he owned the place. She was willing to bet his big, fat truck annoyed everyone in town.

The sudden blast of a car horn made her gasp and slam on her brakes. She hissed in a breath when she realized she had almost driven head on into another car. With an apologetic wave, she veered back to her side of the road.

Dammit, Nick. Look what you made me do.

She knew it wasn't actually his fault, but it was easier to blame him. It figured he'd be in Silverwood. Momentary paranoia led her train of thought down a path where Nick had actually followed her after she mentioned Silverwood, but that was a stretch. The tree farm was close to Silverwood, so he probably worked here. Or lived here. She had to stop being so cynical. It was the part of her brain that stopped trusting people that came to assumptions like that.

Grayson had really done a number on her.

Yes, blame Grayson, she said to herself. *He's the bad guy.*

And she had the emotional scars to prove it.

Chapter Four

The sparkling snow blanketing the ground crunched beneath Holly's thick winter boots as she walked through the town square. It was a sound she had to get used to again, after spending many winters stomping through the slushy city streets. She focused her camera on shop signs and Christmas wreaths, snapping pictures with hopes of getting some kind of inspiration as she hunted down a place to eat.

Inspiration used to come so easily to her. She'd see beautiful, moving images and rush back to her studio to let her visions flow through her paint brush. She'd been flooded with more ideas than she could keep up with. Then, something changed. The last couple years of painting had her creating dark, emotionally charged, abstract work. It was what she was feeling, so she'd gone with it. But those pieces didn't sell. It was as if they were coming from a darker part of herself that no one was interested in seeing.

The whole miserable situation with Grayson wasn't helping matters, either. It had been like a slap in the face when she realized he wasn't bringing her any joy anymore. He was the opposite of supportive, and instead of finding passion and inspiration, she was trapped in a pit of depression and gloom.

No, she had to stop thinking about him. She cleared her throat and shook her head, hoping thoughts of Grayson would disappear.

The center square in Silverwood was like a scene right out of a Christmas card. Every shop, café, and place of business was adorned with garlands of pine, strung with twinkling lights and bright red bows. Silver and gold ornaments dotted every topiary plant along the sidewalks, and holly sprigs highlighted wreaths on every door.

She'd seen the streets of New York decked out for the holidays—sometimes overly so—but this was different. This felt more genuine, like the heart and soul of the town was brought to life in every piece of decoration. The town square breathed Christmas.

She'd taken so many pictures, her camera's low battery light began to flash. As she shut off the camera and placed it back in its case, her stomach grumbled again. Like an answer to its call, the scrumptious scent of baked goods and herbs and spices wafted toward her. She had no choice but to heed its beck and call.

Following the delicious smell, she found the source pretty easily. A glance through the paneled windows of the quaint shop told her the place was quite popular. The shop's name was stenciled in gold foil on the glass door.

The Gingerbread House.

There was a menu set in a frame fastened to the brick wall near the door. A variety of Christmas-themed cupcakes were displayed in the window, each of them sure to invite patrons in with their mouth-watering and creative designs. One had green frosting shaped into a Christmas tree, complete with candy ornaments and a sugar star at its top. Another sported a miniature scene of a fondant penguin in a winter scarf and a hat holding a string of colored lights. Holly found them adorable and could imagine finding it hard to destroy the artistic creations by eating them. The shop wasn't just offering the delectable cupcakes, muffins, and tarts displayed in the windows. They also served a number of lunch items.

"Perfect." Holly smiled as she made her way into the eatery.

It appeared to be a cafeteria-like setting, where customers queued up to a counter to order before having a seat at one of the charming tables. She fell in place at the back of the line, noting the smiles and joy present on the faces of all the patrons and workers. Soaking it all in, she realized she wasn't used to it. Not that New Yorkers weren't jovial. Some of the friendliest people she'd ever met were from New York. Like Kim. But there was something different here. It was as if everyone was connected, a part of something big and meaningful.

The bell above the door startled her from her trance. She did a double take when she realized it was Nick. He lugged a net-wrapped tree behind him and still had a dusting of snow on his coat.

"Oh," she said. *This guy again. Maybe he really is following me.*

"Hey." The smile on his face grew when he realized who she was. "Hello."

"Nick, right?"

"That's right. I'm afraid I didn't catch your name."

"It's Holly." Her eyes went to the tree in his arms. "Making a

26

delivery, I see."

"Uh …Yes. Yeah."

A young man in a green apron came out from behind the counter and approached Nick.

"Hey. Looks like another good one this year." The young man grabbed the netting, taking the tree from Nick.

"Thanks, Darby." Nick used the opportunity of having his hands freed to remove his bomber hat. "Did Viola find the box of decorations?"

"Yeah, she brought it up from the basement. Other than that, the morning delivery came in on time, we got a party order from Mrs. Mills, and that box of muffins was brought over to the police department this morning, just as you requested."

"Great. Thanks."

"Oh, and Jill Harvey called. She needs your approval on the new crepe stand for the Christmas festival."

"I'm on it." Nick gave him a nod. "Great work, Darby."

"No problem, boss. I'll get this set up."

As Darby dragged the tree over to the corner reserved for its presentation, Holly found herself gaping at Nick. He caught her staring, but simply gave her a smile in return.

"Boss? Are you …? So, you're the manager here?" she asked.

Nick stuck his hands in his pockets. "I, uh, own the shop."

"Wow. Okay. And you're in charge of the Christmas festival?"

"I'm the event coordinator, yes."

Holly glanced at the tree in the corner and thought of their encounter that morning. "And you chop down Christmas trees to boot."

"I co-run a tree lot with my sister. It used to be my dad's business, but he's, uh, retired now."

The woman in line in front of Holly turned around, her smile reaching her eyes. "Nick's also an athlete. He beat his own all-time record in the 10k marathon this past fall."

"Oh, stop bragging for me, Allison." A dimple appeared in Nick's cheek. "It was a charity event."

"Which you organized," Allison added.

"Oh, really?" Holly tucked a wave of brunette hair behind her ear. "You seem to be responsible for everything around here."

"No, no. I just do my part. But, yeah, I guess I do have a lot of balls in the air. You'll see when you come to the festival."

Wow, the ego on this guy. Bragging about his balls. I'm surprised he fit his big head through the door.

"Oh, I don't know." Holly gave him a dismissive wave. "I'm not that big on Christmas. Or festivals."

"What?" Nick tilted his head.

"Not big on Christmas?" Allison asked, looking at her over her shoulder with wide eyes. "I don't think I've ever heard of such a thing."

"Come on, Holly." Nick tilted his head, the blue of his eyes gleaming in the light. "Give me a chance. You've got to come. It's the biggest event of the year. There's even a contest the town is entering for the best decorated Christmas tree in the state."

"Cash prize!" Allison added.

Nick dropped his gaze. Allison gave Holly a small smile and then turned back around in line.

"I really wish you'd think about it," Nick said. "Hot chocolate.

Crepes. Churros. The lighting of the big tree. You've got to come."

God, this guy won't let up. "I'll think about it."

"Well, let me show you some Silverwood hospitality to convince you, and uh, to apologize again for the mishap back on the road." He scurried over to an empty table and held out a chair.

"Oh. You don't have to do that."

"Please, I insist. Lunch or dessert?"

Holly bit her cheek. "Um, both?"

He smiled at her. There was that dimple again. "Have a seat. I'll have it brought to your table."

Holly sat down in the chair he offered her.

"Viola!" he called out. "Can you please bring a Silverwood special to table three? And it's on the house."

The brunette woman behind the counter smiled and nodded.

Holly gasped. "No. I can't ask you—"

"It's the least I can do."

She fiddled with her camera strap. "Thank you."

"Don't thank me yet. Have a taste first. It's my own personal favorite."

"Oh."

"I've got to run. Things to do." He gave her a wink. "But I hope to see you around."

He was out the door before she could answer. She found herself watching him go, unable to look away. As he disappeared down the street, Holly felt a flutter in her stomach. But she couldn't tell if it was because of hunger or because of Nick.

Viola came over to her table and placed a small basket of steaming biscuits down in front of Holly.

"Appetizer." Viola smiled at her. "Nick's recipe. Actually, the whole special is."

Holly blinked. "Why am I not surprised? Is there anything he doesn't do?"

"I know, right? He's a jack of all trades."

Holly narrowed her eyes. "Yeah, what's that all about?"

Viola furrowed her brow. "What do you mean?"

"I mean, what's he trying to prove?"

Viola looked confused, tucking a strand of hair behind her ear. "I don't understand."

Oh, no. I've upset her. She's not responsible for Nick. She just got caught in the crossfire.

Holly waved her hand in dismissal. "I'm sorry. It's nothing. I just get grumpy when I'm hungry."

"Oh. All right." Viola's smile returned. "I'll be back with the special in a bit."

"Thank you. Viola, right?"

"Right."

As Viola hurried back to the kitchen, Holly glared at Nick's biscuits. What *was* he trying to prove? And what was with all the bragging? Was she some kind of target in a game he liked to play? Impress the newbie in town so he could take advantage? Or did he really think that highly of himself? She knew all about men like Nick, men who buried themselves in their work, spreading themselves too thin and never having any real time for anyone else. They were always busy feeding their egos and collecting praise about how great they were to let anyone into their lives. Because, otherwise, they'd have to pay attention to someone other than themselves.

No, she didn't buy Nick's good guy, all-around-hero act. There was something he was hiding. As far as she was concerned, Nick was potentially bad news. And she already had her fill of bad news lately.

Chapter Five

Holly pulled into the parking lot of the Silverwood Art School for Children. The red-brick building was a little more than twice the size of her cabin, but from her recollections of the place, she remembered it being huge. The trunk of her car was filled with groceries, but in the cold weather, they would keep long enough for her to stop in and visit her former teacher.

Even pulling the door open was different from what she remembered. When she was younger, she had to use all her might to get the huge, glass-windowed door to budge. It was a testament to how many years she'd been away that she could open it so easily.

Inside, the lobby had been renovated and the furniture had been arranged differently. A new counter had been installed, a beautiful polished oak. The walls were a deep cerulean, making a nice contrast to the white couch and chairs in the waiting area. One wall was filled from floor to ceiling with painted canvases. And one painting in particular caught her eye.

It was something she had made when she was ten, but she would have recognized it anywhere. An acrylic-painted tree was portrayed swaying in the wind, its branches filled with pink flowers. A scattering of pink buds floated on the wind against a background of deep blue with faint swirls of lavender embedded here and there. It had been neatly done, with lighting effects to give it a realistic vibe. Quite impressive for a ten-year-old. Holly smiled, remembering how proud she had been when she made it.

"Hello," came a pleasant female voice from behind her. "Can I help you?"

Holly turned to face a woman who was around her age. The woman's hand rested on a very pregnant belly, and her smile was kind. As Holly took in her features, her eyes began to widen.

"Lucy?"

Lucy's eyes widened at first. But then her smile faded, her jaw tightened, and her eyes narrowed. She took a step back from Holly and crossed her arms over her chest. "Oh, Holly. It's you."

Holly's face fell as she remembered why Lucy was giving her such a cold welcome. Holly and Lucy used to attend art classes together at the school when they were younger. They'd become friends, and their annual meetups at art school became something of a tradition.

When Holly's family stopped coming to Silverwood—right about the same time that Holly was about to head off to college—Holly and Lucy promised each other they'd keep in touch. They both kept their promises over the next few years, but then Holly started to get noticed in the art world. Despite Lucy's emails and text messages of support, Holly got too wrapped up in the excitement of having her art showcased and her new life as an up-and-comer that her promise to Lucy fell to the wayside.

She hadn't meant for it to happen, and seeing the look now

on Lucy's face, Holly regretted not keeping her word.

"I'm surprised to see you in Silverwood." Lucy's voice was flat. She turned and walked toward the reception desk, picking up a pile of papers and flipping thought them as if Holly's presence was no big deal.

"Lucy, it's, uh … It's so good to see you."

Lucy glanced at her for a split second before returning her attention to the papers.

"You work here?" Holly asked.

"Yeah, I do. You'd know that if you'd bothered to answer any of my emails or texts. But hey, I guess big-time art celebrities don't have time for us small-town folk. I'm sure you had more important things to do."

"No, Lucy. It wasn't like that. I—"

"Oh, I'm sorry. I'm super busy right now. You know how it is. So, unless you have some pressing business …?"

Holly swallowed back the shame clogging her throat. "No. I mean … Is Mrs. Weedleman, um, available?"

"She's teaching a class right now. And there's another one due to come in right after that one's done. So you could leave a message, and she'll get back to you. Unlike *some* people, she actually treats others with respect and returns their messages. You know, like a decent human being."

Holly's jaw hung open. She couldn't form words for a moment, only able to cower under the intense glare Lucy was giving her.

Clearing her throat, Holly shook her head. "No, that's all right. I'll, uh, come back another time. Sorry to have … bothered you."

She turned toward the door, forcing herself to steady her pace and not bolt through it in utter humiliation. Her chest felt hollow, as if Lucy had just scraped her heart out of her chest with a fork and left her with an ice-cold gaping hole.

Her mind was so abuzz with the scene that had just played out that she hadn't kept track of her movements. She went through the motions without realizing it, and before she knew it, she was parking her car in front of the cabin.

Her legs felt heavy as she trudged her way inside and threw her keys on the sideboard. She felt awful for losing touch with Lucy, for not answering any of her messages. And she felt childish for not owning up to it and taking responsibility for her actions. Lucy had been kind and supportive, and how did Holly reciprocate? By totally dismissing her. She could just imagine what Lucy thought of her now.

As she finished lighting a fire to chase away the frigid feeling of disgrace, her phone buzzed. She let herself fall onto the couch and tucked her feet under herself as she opened the email notification. Part of her expected it to be from Lucy, finishing her rant and properly telling her off, no holds barred. But when she saw that it was an email from her agent, she sat up and felt the rhythm of her heart speed up.

Dear Holly

I trust you're well and settled in at your holiday retreat.

As we discussed, I'm following up with the

feedback from the recent submission to the Petra Klopf Gallery. I'm afraid the response is the same as our other submissions—it's not the right fit for them.

As you know from our last meeting, this was our last-ditch effort to get your work picked up, and I'm afraid we've hit a wall. I do not believe there is anything more I can do for you, Holly. I believe the time has come to part ways.

I do wish you all the best in your future endeavors.

Regards,
Anita Bledlow

Holly couldn't breathe. She could feel the tears forming but couldn't muster the energy to wipe them away.

Did that really just happen?

Holly threw her phone beside her on the couch and pulled her knees to her chest. She wrapped her arms around her legs and buried her head as the tears came.

Nothing could possibly happen to make things any worse. This was it. Her low point. She was a failure. At everything.

Sniffing back tears, she lifted her head and stared into the fire. How had it come to this? Maybe she had been too ambitious. Maybe she let fame and fortune destroy the decency inside her, and with it her talent. Had she really lost sight of what was really important?

Friends. Family. Simply being kind. Creating for the sake of creating and not for making money.

She raked her fingers through her hair and grunted. No. She wouldn't let go of the good, caring, determined, imaginative person she knew she still was inside. She'd have to get her life back in order. One step at a time, if that's how it had to be. And she was going to start with Lucy, since that was the most prominent situation in her mind at the moment.

After wiping her cheeks dry, she grabbed her phone. She stared at the screen for a second, unsure what to do. She wasn't sure Lucy would even open an email from her. Maybe a direct message of some sort would be better at getting Lucy's attention. Would it be considered stalking if she tracked her down on social media? Cringing, she opened Instagram and typed Lucy's name into the search bar. She was lucky Lucy hyphenated her last name with her husband's, otherwise Holly might not have found her. Lucy's most recently posted picture was only a day old, so Holly felt confident Lucy would be using the app regularly and see her message. Clicking on the message button, Holly began pouring her heart out.

> Lucy, I don't know if you'll even read this, but I have to tell you how sorry I am. It was foolish of me to ignore your messages all these years. I don't know what I was thinking to throw away such a meaningful friendship. It was stupid of me, and I'm extremely sorry. If you can find it in your heart to give me a chance to apologize in person, I promise to never let you down again.

She ended the message by leaving her number, in case Lucy wanted to call or text her directly instead of writing through the app. She hit send and closed the app, telling herself not to get her hopes up that Lucy would give her a second chance. She'd just have to wait and see.

After over an hour of waiting and checking her phone with nothing but silence as a reply, Holly watched the last of the embers in the fireplace die down. With a sigh, she pushed herself off the couch and headed to bed, hoping the next day would mark a fresh beginning, a step in the right direction toward a new and improved life.

Chapter Six

It was still dark outside when Holly awoke the next morning. She hadn't set an alarm, and there was no intrusion of noise, such as a jackhammer tearing up New York City streets or cars honking at each other. Just silence. But she didn't feel the need to sleep any longer. She felt refreshed and rested. Who knew mountain life could relax a person so much? Even after a chaotic and emotionally stressful day. It had only been one night, but Holly was still impressed.

As she stretched, she let out a contented sigh. She laughed, realizing she wasn't even ashamed of making such a noise. The house was silent as she swung her legs over the side of the bed. She slipped on some fuzzy slippers and stood, looking forward to tackling the day.

Grateful she'd stocked up on groceries, she headed to the kitchen to brew some coffee. As the aroma of Arabica beans filled the air, Holly was drawn to the window. The snow stood higher than it did the day before. It was so pure and untouched, like a clean slate. It hit a chord deep inside her. She had had her doubts last night, but now she felt this vacation was exactly what she needed to clear her mind, do some emotional and spiritual healing, and start all over.

She'd just taken her first sip of coffee when her phone buzzed. She realized she hadn't even had the urge to check her email and messages like she usually did every morning in New York.

What's happening to me? she thought with a laugh.

She held her breath for a moment, wondering if Lucy had finally read her message and decided to answer her. One glance at the screenful of emojis told her the message was from Kim. Somewhere in the mix, there was an actual message.

> Holly, it snowed here! I miss our snowball fights.

It was followed by emojis of snowflakes, an explosion, and laughing smilies. Holly figured this was Kim's version of an online snowball fight. She decided to reply with the same emojis to represent her retaliation. Kim's response came immediately.

> OMG HOLLY! How are the mountains treating you?

> Better than I expected!

> That's great! Meet any cute mountain men? Send pictures!

> LOL You know that's not why I'm here, right?

Yeah, yeah. Just answer the question!

Holly's thumb hovered over the phone's keyboard. A part of her wanted to tell Kim about Nick. Buy why? It wasn't as if she was actually interested in him, was she? She'd just met him. And the first meeting could have landed her in the hospital. And sure, he was cute, but that didn't take away from the fact that he was full of himself. Plus, she didn't want to give Kim any ammunition to egg her on.

**Some pretty cute mountain dogs. Does
that count?**

Totally! Definitely send pictures!

Holly was relieved when Kim added a few dog emojis and left it at that. She didn't really want to get into a conversation about not being ready to get back up on the dating horse so soon. Even if Grayson had practically been absent from their relationship for the last six months. If she thought about it that way, then she'd actually been single for a while now.

After a hot, rejuvenating shower, Holly dressed in layers and headed out, prepared to enjoy the beginning of her new journey of figuring out what she wanted for herself. If nothing else, she welcomed the change in scenery.

Just as she was about to step out the door, her phone buzzed again. Preemptively, she smiled, figuring it was Kim coming back with another comment. Instead, she found a message from Lucy.

Her heart began hammering in her chest, and she could feel heat rise in her cheeks. She braced herself for the worst but begged the universe it was Lucy giving her a chance.

> **Fine. We can talk. Come by the school around three.**

Holly's heart swelled. She immediately wrote back.

> **Thank you, Lucy! I'll be there.**

She waited for a minute, shifting her weight back and forth on her feet, but Lucy didn't reply. With a sigh, she tucked her phone away. It was fine. Lucy was giving her a chance to talk, and she was determined to make amends. Three o'clock couldn't come soon enough.

Holly held her breath as she pulled open the door at the art school. It was fifteen minutes until three, but she couldn't wait any longer. She had already spent the day wandering the town and getting reacquainted with the highlights of Silverwood.

No one was at the front desk, but Holly could hear muffled voices coming from one of the classrooms. She decided to sit in the waiting area and calm herself down, going over in her head what she wanted to say to Lucy.

She'd checked the clock on the wall a hundred times before the door to the classroom finally opened. Holly stood, taking a long deep breath and letting it out slowly. Straightening her clothes, she watched as the people from the room emptied out into the hall. The first thing to hit Holly was the noise. Happy squeals and joyful laughter filled the hall as a group of ten children around the ages of seven and eight rushed out. Most of them waved at Lucy, who had been focusing on them so much she hadn't spotted Holly yet.

The children gathered their things and left the building, and when the door finally closed behind them, the building grew silent. Holly waited patiently until Lucy realized she was there. She needed to clear the air with Lucy, but she didn't want to seem pushy.

Lucy gave her a slight nod as she placed some papers on the front counter. "Holly," was all she said.

"Did you want to go somewhere to talk, or—"

"No, we can talk here." Lucy gestured to the couch. "Have a seat."

Her nerves were frazzled. She cleared her throat and sat down again. As soon as Lucy sat down across from her, Holly scooted forward on the couch.

"Lucy, thank you for giving me a chance."

"You can thank Emily—um, Mrs. Weedleman—for that. She's the one who convinced me to bury the hatchet and take the high road."

"She's very wise. I will definitely thank her." Holly swallowed back her nervousness. "I made a big mistake by not keeping in contact with you. I don't know where my head was. I was overwhelmed with everything that was happening—which is not an excuse, I know—and I should have realized you were there for me being a genuine friend."

Lucy huffed a breath through her nose, but her shoulders relaxed a bit. "Yeah, I would have been there for you. You should have known I would have gone to extremes for you. I make a pretty good sounding board, and I would have been your biggest cheerleader. But you never gave me a chance."

Holly pressed her hands to her heart. "I'm so sorry. I wish I could go back and change all that. I didn't see back then how valuable your friendship is, and I just hope I haven't ruined any chance of reconciling it."

Lucy studied her for a moment. "You're lucky these hormones are making me all emotional and sentimental. I want to believe your apology is genuine."

"It is! Oh, Lucy." Holly reached out and grabbed her hand with both of hers. "I'm so sorry. From the bottom of my heart."

Lucy's frown slowly grew into a small smile. "All right. It's Christmas, so in that spirit, you're forgiven. But just know I never forget."

Holly almost whooped with joy as she stood, pulling Lucy with her and gathering her into an embrace. She pulled her close and squeezed her, recalling the many happy memories from when they attended the art school together every winter.

"I can't believe I almost screwed this up." Holly took a step back. "It's amazing to see you. It's been so long."

"Over a decade."

"Feels like forever." Holly let out a small laugh. "And you

work here now. How cool is that?"

"Yeah." Lucy nodded. "I teach a couple classes and pitch in with admin work."

"That's awesome. It must be so fun working with the kids."

"It's the best. But, I mean, it probably pales in comparison to being a famous artist."

"Oh." Holly averted her gaze for a second. "I wouldn't say famous."

Lucy scoffed. "I've got a copy of Entrepreneur Weekly that says differently."

Holly blanched. Despite Lucy having been upset with her, she had still gotten a copy of the magazine Holly had been featured in. "Well, that must be a couple years old."

Lucy shrugged. "So, what brings you to Silverwood? Are you spending Christmas here?"

"Yeah."

Lucy clapped her hands together and smiled. "Just like the old days. Okay, reconciliation plan. We need to catch up. That is, if you don't mind being seen with us common folk."

"Oh, Lucy." Holly offered her a small laugh. "Stop it. Of course we can catch up. I'd love to. I owe it to you. Let's have dinner. Does tomorrow work for you?"

"I think I can fit that into my schedule. Yeah. Besides, I can never turn down an invitation to food."

"That would be great." Holly's gaze slipped down to Lucy's belly. "Okay, I can't hold back anymore. I'm so excited that you're expecting."

With a laugh, Lucy rubbed her belly. "Ready to pop any day

now."

"That's amazing. Congratulations." She leaned in a bit closer. "Are you nervous?"

"Ha! I think my husband is more nervous than I am."

Holly laughed and then looked over her shoulder. "So, is Mrs. Weedleman here?"

"Yeah. She's just finishing up in the back. She'll be out any second now."

As soon as she had said it, a figure moved into the hallway. As the older, black woman came closer, her eyes widened with delight and a smile bloomed upon her face. Mrs. Weedleman had gotten a little more feeble and a lot more gray in the time since Holly last saw her. But her eyes were still filled with kindness, and her smooth, high cheekbones still made Holly think of grace and beauty.

"I thought my ears were ringing." Mrs. Weedleman smiled as she studied her. "Holly St. Ives, I do declare."

A sense of nostalgia overcame Holly as her former art teacher pulled her in for a hug. "Mrs. Weedleman, it's so great to see you."

"Please, dear. We're old friends by now—some of us older than others." She let out a hearty laugh. "Call me Emily."

"All right, Emily." Holly cringed. "That's going to take some getting used to."

"Well, so is looking at you all grown up," Emily said. "If I hadn't been keeping track of your success, I might not have recognized you."

There was an acidic churn in Holly's stomach at the word *success*. "Anything I've achieved was only possible because I had an excellent teacher."

Emily chuckled. "I don't know about that, but it's not every day I get a shout out from a celebrity, so I'm going to take that as a compliment."

"I'm no celebrity. But, yes." Holly placed a hand on Emily's arm. "Please do take it as a compliment, because I meant it."

"Thank you, dear." Emily looked between Holly and Lucy. "I see we've all played nice and made up."

"Yes." Holly gave Lucy a smile. "Thanks for talking her into giving me a chance to apologize."

Lucy lifted a shoulder. "Well, I did lay it into you pretty hard there yesterday. And then once I got that off my chest and was able to sleep on it, I was able to really take Emily's advice."

"You should always take my advice," Emily said. "I'm sure I'm the smartest woman you know."

"It's true," Holly said as they all laughed.

"So, are you in Silverwood for Christmas?" Emily asked Holly.

"Yeah, but just me." Holly tucked a strand of hair behind her ear. "My mom went back to the Philippines to stay with my aunt, and my dad …"

Emily took her hand. "Oh, honey, I heard about his passing. I was so sorry to hear about it."

"Me too, Holly," Lucy chimed in. "I remember crying when I heard the news. And I almost wrote you, but …"

Holly let out a slow breath and placed a hand on Lucy's arm. "Thank you for that."

"But you spending time here in Silverwood sure does please my heart so." Emily tilted her head. "It would please it even more if you'd settle down here for good."

"Oh, yeah!" Lucy beamed at Holly, her eyes lighting up. "I'd love that too. It would totally make up for you ghosting me all those years."

"Well, we'll see." Holly smiled at them both and then turned her attention to the school, admiring the new layout. "The place looks great, by the way."

Emily followed her gaze. "Yeah, we renovated a few years ago."

"More like five," Lucy said.

"Has it been that long?" Emily let out a soft chuckle. "Why, yes, it has. We hired an interior designer to give us some tips. I'm pretty pleased with how things turned out."

"It's modern yet still has that cozy, warm-hearted touch to it. I love it." Holly pointed to the wall covered with art. "I'm especially fond of the feature wall."

"Me too." Lucy shuffled over and pointed to a painting of what was supposed to be a horse eating in a field. "Remember this one? You made so much fun of me for the color of the horse."

"I did not," Holly replied with a laugh. "It just looked a little purple to me. It kind of still does."

Lucy narrowed her eyes, pretending she was insulted. "It's shadowing, Holly."

Holly couldn't stop smiling, remembering how she and Lucy used to rile each other up over art. It was never serious, all in good fun. And they always ended up laughing until they cried.

"You're right." Holly raised her hands in defeat. "And the painting looks perfect up on the wall."

"You two and your bickering," Emily said, shaking her head.

"Emily, would it be okay for me to see the classrooms?" Holly asked.

"Of course." Emily held her arm out, directed down the hall. "Let's have a tour."

A thrill ran through Holly as they made their way to the first classroom.

The air was filled with the scent of oil-based paint, the woody aroma of charcoal pencils, and the bitter smell of linseed-oil-soaked canvas. The memories flooded her. In just a couple whiffs, Holly was transported back to her childhood days, back to a simpler time when she was passionate about creating art without giving a second thought about if what she created was something that would sell. How she wished she would go back to that mindset and create freely.

Emily opened the first door on the left. "We did major renovations on the classrooms, practically tearing down the external walls and installing these large windows to bring in more natural light."

"Looks amazing." Holly made her way around the classroom, running her fingers along the paint brushes sitting in cups of water and the lined-up bottles of tempera paint. The art tables and easels were a lot smaller than she remembered, but the memories were still there.

She smiled and turned to Lucy. "Do you remember the paper mâché fight we got into?"

Lucy's eyes widened as she let out a laugh. "Oh, yeah! Oh, that was crazy. I think I had to throw away the blouse I was wearing, it was so ruined."

"That's nothing," Holly said. "I had hardened plaster in my hair and my mom had to cut it out."

"Not to mention the mess you two left me," Emily added.

The three of them fell into a chorus of laughter, and Holly felt her heart warm. She had made the right choice reaching out to Lucy. At least in this area of her life, things were as they should be.

"So many great memories of this place." Holly glanced around the room again.

"Those memories are what built this place." Emily clasped her hands together. "I'll bring them with me wherever I go."

"Oh, right." Holly gave a slight pout. "I heard you're going to retire."

"Yes, I'm not as young as I used to be." Emily sighed. "My bones are getting weary, and I can't quite hold a paintbrush as still as I should. Not to mention I feel like a nap every couple hours." She laughed as she winked at them.

"What will happen to the school?" Holly asked.

"I haven't exactly decided yet, but I have my feelers out for someone to take over. There's actually someone coming in a few days to take a look at the place."

"That's great, but what about Lucy?"

Lucy rubbed her round belly. "I don't know if I'll be able to fit it into my schedule, otherwise I'd jump at the chance."

As they stepped back into the hall, the front door opened. A little boy with a green knit cap walked in.

"Hi, Mrs. Weedleman. Hi, Lucy," he said as he slipped off his backpack.

"Hey, Eric." Lucy gave him a wave before turning to Holly.

"Our next class is about to start."

"Do you have time to stay?" Emily asked. "Sit in on a class and relive a precious part of your childhood?"

"I would love to," Holly said. "But I'm going to have to take a raincheck."

"All right. I'm going to hold you to that raincheck." Emily embraced her once more. "It's so good to see you."

"You too, Mrs. Wee—Emily."

Emily laughed.

"And don't forget our plans tomorrow night," Lucy added, giving Holly a hug as well. "Otherwise, you'll have to face the wrath."

"I promise I won't forget."

"Good. I'll message you."

"Sounds good." Holly gave them a nod. "It was really great seeing you both."

Emily and Lucy waved and then turned around to get back to work. As Holly opened the front door, she glanced over her shoulder, taking in the school once more. She was left with a feeling of emptiness, as if she'd let go of something dear to her, and her heart wanted it back.

Chapter Seven

Holly wasn't sure why she'd opened up the email from her former agent. Maybe she needed to read it a couple hundred more times until it actually sank in. Nobody wanted her. Not the galleries, not her agent. She felt like a helpless, abandoned puppy left on the side of the road.

Why am I torturing myself? She asked herself as she closed her laptop. Raking her fingers through her hair, she took a deep breath and told herself she needed to get her mind off her troubles. She marched to her closet to pick out a weather-appropriate outfit so she could get out of the cabin and submerge herself in the natural habitat of the Silverwood locals.

An hour later she was ready to go and about to put her car in reverse and pull away from the house when her phone buzzed. She smiled when she saw Lucy's name on the screen.

I know just the place for dinner tonight.
I'll send you the address.

Sounds great! Can't wait!

Also, they're starting to set up the
festival. Crepes galore! You should check
it out.

The sun was high in the sky when she got to the town square, and the festival setup was in full swing. Holly's jaw dropped at the amount of stands and decorations that had already filled the square overnight. It made her think of little elves rushing in to help out while everyone was asleep—and not just because there were actual people dressed in elf costumes doing the setup. It was all so magical. Everyone was smiling as they worked together to stock and decorate their stands. There was a cheery atmosphere created by Christmas music being played over loudspeakers. Near the center of the square, there stood an actual North Pole, and not far off, a crane was in the process of erecting the festival's Christmas tree.

"Easy, Bobby!"

Holly recognized the voice as Nick's. She walked a little closer, noting how Nick ran a hand over his hair as he stretched his neck. He called out a few more directions to the team getting the tree in place, and Holly couldn't help but admire his leadership skills.

An echoing bark roused her from her daze, and she took a step back when an Alaskan Malamute raced her way.

"Oh," she exclaimed, unsure what to do.

The dog stopped by her feet, panting as it studied her, and then began sniffing her boots.

Hesitating for a second, Holly crouched down and pet the dog's head. "Hey. Hi, there, Cupid."

A little girl, who ran up behind the dog, let out a giggle. "That's not Cupid."

"It's not?" Holly tilted her head. "I could have sworn …"

"His name is Dasher. He's my dog. One of Cupid's brothers."

The girl looked to be about eight or nine and had wavy brunette hair stuffed beneath a white, wooly hat.

"Cupid is my son's dog," said a portly older man with a thick white beard, approaching them. "Hi, I'm Nicholas Mason."

"Oh, hi. It's nice to meet the man who fathered such a diligent worker."

"Ah, you know my Nicky?"

Nicky? She held back a giggle. "Yeah, we met. He seems to be doing everything in Silverwood."

Mr. Mason nodded. "That he does."

"I like your boots," the little girl said. Her smile was full of sunshine.

"Oh, thank you," Holly said. "They're new."

"I'm Avery. What's your name?"

"I'm Holly."

"That's a pretty name."

"Thank you. So is Avery. I think you're the very first Avery I ever met."

Avery beamed. A loud bark interrupted their discussion, and Holly turned to see Dasher bounding towards some elves transporting a plastic deer.

"Dasher, wait!" Avery called, taking off after him.

"Don't go too far, Avery!" Mr. Mason called.

"I won't, Grandpa!"

"I'm an old man," Mr. Mason mumbled. "I can't walk as fast

as you."

Holly watched the girl as her words sunk in. *Grandpa?*

"Is Avery … Nick's daughter?"

"Oh, ha ha ha! No, dear."

Holly could have sworn his laugh sounded more like *ho ho ho.* Especially when he placed his hands on his jiggling belly as he chuckled.

"No," Mr. Mason tucked his gloved hands into his coat pockets. "Avery is my daughter Rachel's kid."

Right. Nick had mentioned he had a sister. "Ah, okay. So, Avery is his niece."

"Yes." He watched her keep up with Dasher, who chased a squirrel across the square until it ran up a tree.

What was it with those dogs and squirrels?

"Avery's a good kid," Mr. Mason continued. "And smart as a whip for her age too."

"And she's got impeccable taste in boots." Holly gave him a wink.

Mr. Mason chuckled, his hands on his round belly.

The air grew a little quieter when the motor of the crane shut off.

"Good work, guys!" Nick called out from his position in front of the now fully upright tree.

Ordinarily, one's eyes would naturally gravitate to the enormous evergreen in the center of the square. But Holly found herself staring at Nick. He walked up to each of his team members and shook their hands and patted them on their backs. After watching him for a moment, Holly felt eyes trained on her. She turned her head to find Mr. Mason smiling at her.

"It's a nice tree." Holly cleared her throat when her sentence ended in nervous laughter.

"Uh-huh." Mr. Mason's grin didn't falter.

There was no fooling him.

"I hear it's going to be entered in a state-wide decorating contest."

Mr. Mason dropped his gaze and adjusted his scarf. "You heard right. The whole town's excited about it."

"Sounds fun." She smiled, hoping he'd forgotten about her little staring episode.

Mr. Mason stepped closer to her. "You know, my Nicky … He's single." He topped off his statement with a wink of his own.

Holly's eyes widened. "Mr. Mason, are you trying to play matchmaker?"

Once again, his hands landed on his belly as he let out a chortle. "Just mentioning the facts."

She bit her cheek, her eyes trained on the ground.

"Hey, I saw that The Gingerbread House's hot chocolate stand is open." Mr. Mason had obviously noticed her embarrassment and decided to change the subject. "How about we test it out? My treat."

"That sounds amazing. I'd love to."

He offered her his arm, and she hooked hers through. As he led the way, she glanced over at Nick. This time, he was looking at her.

"Looks like we've been caught," Mr. Mason joked.

Holly felt a blush bloom in her cheeks. She raised a glove and waved at Nick. He returned the wave.

The hot chocolate stand looked like a mug of hot chocolate, complete with marshmallows on the roof.

"Hey, Mr. Mason," the woman at the counter said. "What'll it be?"

"Two double luscious hot chocolates, please, Viola."

Holly noticed Mr. Mason's hand shake slightly as he handed Viola some bills.

"Coming right up," Viola said.

Holly remembered she was the same woman who'd brought her the lunch special Nick ordered for her.

Avery ran up to join them. "Hey, what about me?"

Mr. Mason chuckled. "Make that three, Viola."

"You got it," she replied.

"So." Holly raised a brow at Mr. Mason. "Nicky?"

Mr. Mason's smile widened. "Called him that when he was a boy. He preferred it to *Junior*. I guess I can't break the habit, even if he's outgrown it."

One of the stand workers came out through a side door and set a bowl of water on the ground. Dasher pranced over and drank from it. Holly marveled at how considerate everyone in Silverwood was. As she watched Dasher drink, an identical dog sidled up next to him and drank. Their heads were so close together, Holly wasn't sure where one dog ended and the other began.

"Is that Cupid?" Holly asked Mr. Mason.

"Sure is," came a voice from behind them.

Holly turned to find Nick. She found herself flustered as he got closer. Out of the corner of her eye, Holly spotted Viola handing

Mr. Mason the hot chocolates he'd ordered. Viola placed his directly into his hands, waiting until he had a proper hold of it before letting go.

"Hi, Holly." Nick nodded at her. "Glad you decided to come see the festival."

Holly offered him a small smile. She still wasn't buying his hero act, but she didn't want to seem rude in front of his father and niece.

Nick's eyes flitted over her face. "I see you've met my family."

"I sure did, *Nicky*." Holly bit back a laugh.

Nick cringed, sucking in air through his teeth. "Dad."

"Oh, Nicky." Mr. Mason chuckled. "Don't bust my chops."

Nick ran a hand over his beard and switched his attention back to Holly. "And I see you've met Dasher as well."

"Yes, I have." Holly took her hot chocolate mug from Mr. Mason. "I mistook him for his brother. But Avery set me straight. I'm amazed you can tell them apart."

"You should see the nine of them together." Nick said, motioning to Viola for another hot chocolate and placing money on the counter.

"It's like a moving mountain of fur." Avery extended her arms and widened her eyes.

"That's got to be a sight to see," Holly said.

"Oh, that's nothing," Nick said. "You should hear them."

"You want to hear them?" Avery asked, whipped cream sticking to her upper lip.

"No, Avery, let's not—"

Before Nick could finish his sentence, Avery stuck her chin in the air and let out a howl that sounded like a wolf's call.

Cupid and Dasher immediately turned their heads to her, and in a matter of seconds joined her with their own howls. Holly couldn't believe how loud they were. Their calls echoed through the town square, and Holly believed it was ricocheting off the mountains and traveling across the state.

But it wasn't just echoes. She could distinctly make out a few different pitches of the call, and she knew they must be from Cupid's and Dasher's siblings.

Everyone in the square was watching them. Nick's face grew red with embarrassment.

He gently put a hand on Avery's shoulders. "Okay, that's enough. If they don't stop, their brothers and sisters are going to come running."

"From their homes?" Holly asked.

"You think I'm kidding, I know," Nick said as he, Avery, and Mr. Mason calmed down Cupid and Dasher. "They've got a really strong bond. The first time it happened we were all baffled. We'd never seen anything like it. Then it happened a couple more times and we figured it out. We try to not let them go too long howling to avoid a stampede of Alaskan Malamutes charging through Silverwood."

"It's crazy, but true," Mr. Mason added, petting Dasher's chest to calm him down.

Nick appeared to have a death grip on his mug of hot chocolate, so Holly decided to veer the conversation in another direction in hopes he'd feel less self-conscious.

"By the way, I really enjoyed that lunch special. It was

amazing." She waited to see his reaction, betting he loved the compliment.

"Yeah?" he asked, a charming smile surfacing.

"Absolutely. That was your own recipe, right?"

"Yes." He beamed. "Well, it's a variation of my mother's recipe."

"Well, my compliments to the chef. Or the … recipe writer?"

Nick and Holly laughed.

"Thank you," he replied.

"Well, I think Avery and I can leave you two." Mr. Mason placed his empty mug on the counter of the hot chocolate stand. "Finish up, Avery. I've got to get you to art class."

"Oh, at the Silverwood Art School for Children?" Holly asked.

"Yes," Mr. Mason replied. "You know it?"

"I used to go there myself when I was her age," Holly said. "I know Emily. Um, Mrs. Weedleman. The owner. And Lucy."

"Wonderful." Mr. Mason adjusted his scarf. "Small world."

"Hey, thanks for the hot chocolate, Mr. Mason." Holly touched his sleeve.

"My pleasure, Holly. You have fun now."

"Thanks."

"Bye, Holly," Avery called, waving to her.

"Bye." Holly waved back and watched as Dasher followed Avery and Mr. Mason out of the square.

"So, you went to the art school when you were younger?" Nick asked. "I didn't know you used to live in Silverwood."

"Oh, no." Holly shook her head. "I didn't. My family just vacationed here practically every winter."

"So, you've actually been to Silverwood's Christmas Festival before."

"Vaguely. I don't remember it being this big." She glanced around. "Maybe it was just a lot smaller back then."

"The committee has made a few changes and additions."

"Which you're in charge of, right?"

He gave her a sideways look. "Yeah? Why do I feel like you're questioning me as if I've committed a felony?"

"Am I?" She took a sip of her hot chocolate. "I don't know. I'm just wondering what your story is."

"My story?"

She shrugged. "Yeah. Why are you working so hard? What's in it for you?"

He smiled, which surprised her. She thought he might get upset and defend himself. "You ever hear of the joy of giving?"

She narrowed her eyes. "So all this, everything that you do for the town, is because it gives you some kind of thrill?"

Nick shook his head, still smiling. "I guess you don't know the feeling, otherwise you wouldn't be asking me."

"What? No. Just because I don't hold down ten jobs doesn't mean I don't know what it's like to be charitable. I give back."

"Oh, really?" Nick tilted his head. "What do you do for a living?"

She opened her mouth and immediately snapped it shut. She hid behind her hot chocolate, taking a drink while averting her gaze. "I'm in between jobs," she mumbled.

Nick studied her for a moment. "All right. I get that. Speaking of which." Nick placed his empty mug on the counter. "I need to get back. But I'm glad you stopped by. You should come back and see it at night when it's in full swing and all the lights are set up."

"Maybe I will." Holly gave him a half shrug. "But not tonight. I'm meeting an old friend for dinner."

He studied her for a moment and nodded. "Raincheck?"

"You got it."

Chapter Eight

Holly coughed as dust from the box she carried drifted into her face. This was the fourth box she retrieved from the attic, and there were still a dozen more stuffed up there. There was no way she'd be able to go through them all in one day, but she might as well begin the process. She hadn't decided if she definitely wanted to sell the cabin, but either way, she needed to go through the stored-away items and figure out what needed to be donated, sold, or tossed in the trash.

She found an area in the living room to sit, surrounded by the four boxes. She had a coffee nearby, as well as a bowl of popcorn, just in case she started feeling snacky. Letting out a sigh, she tore off the tape from the first box and dug in. A blustery wind howled outside, but luckily Holly had a nice fire going to keep her warm inside.

At the top of the box, she found an old camera wrapped in tissue paper. A warm feeling engulfed her as she cradled it in her hands. It was her first single-lens reflex camera. Her father had spent a fortune on it, but he'd known how much Holly loved art and wanted to support her interests. He'd taken her out and taught her how to use the camera and then, later, how to make sketches of the things she'd photographed.

The next item she pulled out of the box was a small photo album. She flipped through the pages, admiring all the shots her younger self had taken. She'd been a lot more free-spirited with her choice of subject and scenery. Lately, though her skills had improved, she was far too critical, practically to the point where she overthought every aspect and ended up not getting any pictures at all. She needed to be open, more like young Holly.

She had perused a few more albums when the doorbell rang, stirring her from her thoughts and memories. She dusted off her jeans and climbed over the boxes and the pile of albums to answer the door. Peering through the side window, she found Mrs. Miranelli holding a white box decorated with red polka dots and a green ribbon.

Holly opened the door. "Hi, Mrs. Miranelli."

"Holly St. Ives," Mrs. Miranelli said cheerily, "I've got a delivery for you." She shivered as the wind tousled her hair.

"Come in out of the cold. That wind is brutal."

"Thank you, dear." Mrs. Miranelli waddled into the house and pulled off her scarf, sending a scattering of snowflakes floating to the floor. She set down the box she was carrying on a side table and glanced around as if she were searching for something. "Oh, honey. Where's your tree?"

"I, uh, don't know if I'm getting one."

"But, Holly, it's tradition. Your parents always had a beautiful tree every year."

"Maybe I will. We'll see." Holly pointed to the box Mrs.

Miranelli had set down. "What's this?"

"Oh, right!" Mrs. Miranelli handed her the box. "Do you know The Gingerbread House? It's that cute little lunch and dessert place in town."

"As a matter of fact, I do. I sort of know the owner." Holly ignored the heat in her cheeks.

"You do? How?"

"Well, it's kind of a long story. I sort of ran into him—or his dog. Or nearly did. In any case, there was an incident with Nick, and he wanted to apologize by treating me to the lunch special, which was absolutely delicious."

"Well, well, well." Mrs. Miranelli giggled. "This whole story is turning out to be delicious."

"Oh, don't read anything into it." Holly clutched the box against her body. "He was just being nice."

"Well, Nick asked me to bring this to you."

"What? Why?" Holly lifted the lid to peek inside. She found four carefully packaged cupcakes inside. Each of them seemed to have a unique Christmas theme. The scents of vanilla and almond paste and peppermint wafted up to greet her nose.

"It's his Lip-Smacking Cupcake Sampler," Mrs. Miranelli explained.

"But I didn't order this."

"It's a Welcome-To-Silverwood gift. He heard we were neighbors and insisted I bring these to you when I stopped in his shop today. You have to try them." Mrs. Miranelli pointed to the white and green cupcake with a miniature candy cane stuck on top. "The white chocolate mint is my favorite."

"They look amazing. Yeah. I'll give them a try."

Mrs. Miranelli smiled and looked over to the pile of boxes on Holly's floor. "Looks like you're keeping yourself busy."

Holly sighed. "Oh, yeah, I need to go through these boxes and figure out what to do with all this stuff. If I decide to sell the place, I'll need to clear everything out and probably get rid of almost everything in it."

Mrs. Miranelli furrowed her brow. "I do hope you decide to stay. Or at least keep this place for the holidays. This lovely cabin will do so much more for you than that big, scary city."

Holly wasn't sure what to say. She doubted Mrs. Miranelli had stepped foot out of Silverwood, no less venture out to New York. She smiled politely and nodded. "Thanks, Mrs. Miranelli. I'll keep that in mind."

"You do that, dear." Mrs. Miranelli patted her shoulder and then proceeded to check her watch. "Well, I better get back to Henry. If I leave him alone too long, he sneaks into the snack cabinet. I swear he was a racoon in a past life."

With a chortle, Mrs. Miranelli waved a goodbye to her and let herself out. Holly could still hear her humming a Christmas tune as she made her way down Holly's walkway.

Holly took one more look at the cupcakes inside the box. Aside from the white chocolate peppermint one Mrs. Miranelli raved about, there was a red one with the words Merry Christmas written on top of it with white frosting, surrounded by tiny white snowflakes, a cool blue one with a sugar polar bear holding a pot of poinsettias, and a white one sprinkled with chocolate flakes featuring a little gingerbread man wearing a Santa hat.

Remembering that she was going out with Lucy to dinner that evening, Holly decided to stick the entire box in the refrigerator for later.

The pile of boxes and albums on the floor in the living room caught her eye. She sighed, knowing she couldn't just leave them there. A little voice in her head—she suspected it was her mom's—told her to at least go through half of the boxes to get them done and out of the way. After sipping her cup of coffee for energy, she returned to her place in the middle of the box fort and opened the next box.

Her brow furrowed when she realized the contents weren't familiar to her. In particular, an old shoebox that was filled to the brim with envelopes made her extremely curious. Upon opening a few of them, she realized they were love letters her parents had sent each other when they were dating.

There had been a period of time when her parents had had a long-distance relationship. Her father had been in the Philippines for work when he met Holly's mother. They had gotten to know each other, and sparks began to fly, but Holly's father had to return to the states. So, they'd decided to keep in touch via letters, being that this took place pre-internet and cell phone times. Their relationship blossomed, and Holly's father traveled back to the Philippines, determined to marry Holly's mother and ask her to move to the states with him. It was a real-life happily-ever-after love story. And Holly held all the heartfelt words of love in her hands.

One envelope in particular stood out to her. It was big and a shiny white, glittering in the light. Inside, written in calligraphy and signed by her father, was a beautiful poem, asking Holly's mom to marry him. The words brought tears to her eyes. There were no addresses written on the envelope, so Holly assumed her father had given it to her mother in person. She could just imagine him handing it to her and then kneeling down on one knee with a ring box in his hand. The vision was as clear as day to her.

Holly held the envelope to her chest, feeling a small ache. They'd been so much in love, but now her mother was left alone. She closed her eyes, feeling like the world had slowed down its spinning, like she couldn't breathe.

Taking a deep breath, Holly told herself to keep going. She'd grieved her father, and she knew he wouldn't have wanted her to sit here feeling sad. She set the envelope aside and carried on with her task.

Also in the box were a pile of pictures which hadn't made it into any albums. Holly's brow wrinkled at one of them, so she picked it up to study it more closely. In the picture, her parents, dressed in thick coats and hats and scarves, had their arms around each other. Behind them was a shop window, and in the shop's display cases were a number of appetizing cupcakes. Above them, the shop's sign was partially covered, but she could just manage to make out the name: The Gingerbread House.

Chapter Nine

Holly removed her fleece-lined pea coat and draped it over her arm. Straightening her dress, she glanced around the entrance of *Le Ruban Rouge* wondering if she'd arrived before Lucy. When a waving arm caught her eye, she smiled and walked up to Lucy, who was sitting at the bar sipping her drink through a tiny straw.

"You look nice," Lucy said, shoving a pretzel from the bar in her mouth.

"Oh, thanks. So do you."

"That's kind of you. I'm sure that's not why the men at the end of the bar were staring at me though." Lucy rubbed her belly and held up her glass. "They were probably trying to figure out if this was water or something stronger."

"Really?" Holly followed Lucy's gaze and found the two men who were keeping tabs on Lucy.

"It's water!" Lucy assured them.

The men averted their eyes. Holly couldn't hold back a laugh.

A tall, lean man in a white button-down shirt and red tie approached them with a friendly smile. "Hi, Lucy. Your table is ready."

"Thanks, Shane." Lucy smiled at Holly and circled her belly. "We're starving."

Holly admired the main floor of the restaurant, which had a wide L-shaped staircase leading to another floor. The restaurant itself had low-key lighting, but it was offset by the Christmas lights hung along the pillars and walls. The tables were set with white linen tablecloths, adorned with red cloth napkins, candles, and centerpieces of fresh flowers. Christmas wreathes decorated the walls, and a well-lit Christmas tree could be seen on the glass-wall-enclosed balcony that overlooked a frozen lake.

"This place is so charming," Holly said.

"I love it," Lucy said. "It's my favorite."

They were seated at a quaint table for two, and the scent of fresh Casablanca lilies mixed with the aroma of spices and herbs in the air.

"Thanks, Shane," Lucy said to their seater.

"Your waiter will be right with you," Shane said.

"Is it Marcus?" Lucy asked.

"Yes!"

"Oh, perfect. I've been meaning to ask how his classes are going." Lucy smiled at Shane as he nodded and left the table. She turned back to face Holly. "Marcus is my cousin. Do you remember him?"

"I don't think I do," Holly answered.

Lucy narrowed her eyes. "Do you recall a snotty little kid running all over the place when my aunt used to pick me up from art school?"

"Hmm, vaguely."

"Well, that was Marcus. He's in college now and working here part time."

"College?" Holly blew out a breath. "Now I feel old."

Lucy laughed. "Tell me about it."

Holly opened her menu. "What do you recommend?"

"This place is so good, you could literally order anything, and it would be the best thing you ever ate."

"Seriously? That's high praise." Holly perused the entrees. "So I could just close my eyes and point and it would be a winner?"

"Honestly? Yes. And if you don't end up eating it, I definitely would."

After Holly made her decision, she looked around. The patrons all looked pleased with their meals, enjoying their company and the cozy atmosphere. The light jazz playing over the sound system caught her ear. It wasn't overwhelming, but loud enough to add to the pleasant feel of the place.

"It's so good to go someplace and not hear Christmas music," Holly said.

Lucy tilted her head, listening. "Actually, I'm pretty sure this is a jazz rendition of Good King Wenceslas."

Holly listened for a moment and then let out a small laugh. "Oh, wow. You're right. There's no escaping Christmas around here, is there?"

"Who would want to?"

Holly offered a small smile, grateful that the waiter had appeared so she wouldn't have to answer.

"Marcus!" Lucy wiggled herself to standing and embraced her

cousin. "How are you?"

"Good, Lucy." Marcus looked her over. "Oh, wow. Look at you. When are you due?"

"Supposed to be a New Year's baby. But we'll see. How's college?"

"Exhausting." Marcus shook his head. "I'm so glad it's Christmas break."

"Do you remember Holly?" Lucy asked him. "She used to take art classes with me when we were kids."

Marcus shook Holly's hand. "Sorry, no. I think I had some attention problems back then."

"Nice to meet you, Marcus," Holly said. "And no worries. I can barely remember last week, let alone a decade ago."

After their small talk, Lucy and Holly placed their orders. Lucy leaned closer, setting her elbow on the table and resting her chin on her hand.

"So, tell me. Are you dating anyone?"

Holly wasn't sure she wanted to get into the story about Grayson, but there was something about Lucy that made her feel open to talk.

"I was," Holly began. "We went out for a couple years. But the relationship started to become toxic, and so, I broke up with him."

"Well, it sounds to me like you dodged a bullet." She waved a hand.

"I guess you could say that."

"Not that you need a man to make you complete, but if that's what you're looking for, I'm sure your Mister Right is bound to come into your life exactly when he means to."

Holly smirked at her. "That's a very positive attitude."

"It's the only one you'll need."

Movement near the entrance of the restaurant caught her eye. Holly did a double-take when she realized it was Nick walking in with a beautiful woman. She watched them as they were shown to their table. Nick held the chair out for the woman so she could take a seat. They smiled at each other, and Nick said something that made the woman laugh.

There was a strange twisting feeling in Holly's stomach. She shifted in her seat and convinced herself it was just hunger. Besides, she wasn't interested in Nick. He was bad news.

"Holly St. Ives," Lucy said.

Holly finally tore her eyes away from Nick to find Lucy watching her. "What?"

Lucy lowered her voice. "Are you staring at Nick Mason?"

Holly's neck and cheeks grew hot. "What? No. You know him? I'm not staring."

Lucy bit back a laugh. "Everyone knows Nick. He's like the glue that holds this town together."

"I've noticed. Well, it's good to see he takes some time off for a date."

"A date?" Lucy laughed, practically snorting. "Oh, no, no."

"What? He's not with that woman?"

"No, that's his sister Rachel."

"Rachel." Relief flooded Holly's blood, her blush fading away and her stomach knot loosening. "Right. Avery's mom."

"Oh, you *have* been doing some homework. Good for you."

"So, does he ..." Holly cleared her throat and lowered her

voice. "Does he have a girlfriend?"

Lucy raised an eyebrow.

Holly felt the heat rush back into her cheeks. "Oh, you know what? Never mind. I'm not interested. I mean I just got out of a relationship, and I need to take some time to find myself again and—"

"No, I don't think so."

Holly blinked. "What?"

"I don't think he has a girlfriend. Not that I know of. He keeps real busy and spends a lot of time with his family."

"Well that's sweet."

Lucy gave her a half shrug. "Not everyone agrees with you— it's why things didn't work out with his last girlfriend. She was a bit selfish, wanted him all to herself and thought he spent too much time with his dad and his sister's family. Totally jealous of them. So, they broke up."

I knew it. He doesn't make time for anyone else. Well, except his family. But maybe that's because they're the ones singing his praises the loudest, so he keeps them close on purpose.

"So, was this recent?" Holly asked.

Lucy pursed her lips, thinking. "No, maybe a year ago."

Holly nodded, glancing at Nick. He laughed at something Rachel said, and Holly couldn't help but notice how handsome he looked. *No, don't fall for it, she told herself.* "I mean, not that it matters. Why would I care if he's single? It doesn't make any difference to me whether he's in a relationship or not, because I am definitely not interested. Nope."

Lucy simply sat smiling at her.

"Lucy, stop," Holly said with a laugh. "Let's change the subject. Do you know the gender of the baby yet? Or is it a secret?"

That seemed to do the trick. Lucy's expression changed from a devious plotter to a warm-hearted mother. "It's a girl. Sean and I are so excited!"

"That's awesome. Do you have baby names picked out?"

"We do! But we haven't told anyone yet, so mum's the word. But hey, if you're still here by New Year's, you're sure to find out."

"Great. I'll be here for New Year's, and I'm excited to meet the little one."

"Are you headed back to New York right after the holidays?"

Holly let out a long breath. "I haven't decided yet. I'm not obligated to be back, unless one of the galleries in New York changes their mind and decides to take my work into consideration."

"I read about all your showings." Lucy sipped her water. "Those high-profile gallery openings and galas—sounds so exciting. The most exciting thing here are the occasional bears wandering in to steal something."

Holly's eyes widened. "Bears?"

"Oh, it's not often. But it's not unheard of."

Out of the corner of her eye, Holly noticed someone approaching. She had hoped it was their food, but she was surprised to find it was Nick. Holly forced herself not to gasp. She sat up straighter and returned his smile as he made his way to their table."

"Holly, hi. You, uh, you look really nice."

She tucked a strand of hair behind her ear, trying to ignore the sudden acceleration of her heartbeat. "Thanks, Nick. So do you. You clean up well."

"Hello, Lucy."

"Hey, Nick."

His sister was suddenly beside him. Holly smiled at her.

"This is my sister Rachel," Nick said.

Holly stood and shook her hand. "Hi, Rachel. Nice to meet you."

"Nice to finally meet you," Rachel said.

Nick elbowed her and averted his gaze.

"Finally?" Lucy asked.

Nick cleared his throat.

"Oh, um—" Rachel glanced between Nick and Holly. "Avery told me she met you at the Christmas festival."

"Oh, yes. Avery." Holly nodded. "She's so sweet."

"Thanks."

"Excuse me," Marcus interrupted, holding a tray of food.

"Oh, yay!" Lucy exclaimed, clapping her hands a little.

Holly smiled at her friend's excitement. Rachel and Nick took a step back to give Marcus room to do his job.

It was like a cloud of serenity surrounding Holly as the aroma of the food reached her nostrils. Marcus took great care in making sure everything they'd ordered was placed neatly on the table. Holly's mouth watered as her dish was put before her. Presentation alone was making her want to give the place five stars on every restaurant review site.

"Oh, you got the Duck Confit," Rachel remarked to Lucy. "It's one of my favorites."

"So yummy, right?" Lucy said.

"Yes," Rachel said. "I've been begging Pierre for the recipe, but he won't let up."

"Speaking of which." Nick rubbed at the back of his neck. "Did you get a chance to try any of those cupcakes I sent over?"

"Not yet," Holly answered. "I'm saving them for dessert. But you didn't have to do that."

"Sure I did. Didn't you know I'm head of the welcoming committee?"

"Of course you are." Holly let out a small laugh. "Thank you. It was a very nice gesture."

"He made them himself," Rachel said. "Decorated each one by hand, as well."

Nick averted his gaze, looking embarrassed.

"That's impressive," Holly said.

"Just something I do." He shrugged.

Rachel began to contradict him, but Nick elbowed her again, clearing his throat.

"Well, we'll let you get to your dinner," he said to Holly and Lucy. "It was nice seeing you again, Holly."

"You too."

Lucy was quiet for a moment while they ate. Then she leaned forward and whispered, "He's cute, right?"

"What?"

"What? You're single. He's single."

"Lucy, I told you. I'm just here on vacation for the holidays. I'm probably going back to New York. Maybe. I don't know. I'm not sure what I'm doing."

"All right. Well, you're doing the right thing, taking time to figure things out—because you're clearly a bit mixed up. But there's nothing like a quiet cabin in a wintery wonderland to clear your mind and figure out what you want."

Holly sighed. "Yeah. I hope so."

"You're coming to the school and sitting in on a class, right? It would be so fun to have you there."

"Of course."

"Do you still take pictures?"

"I do." Holly narrowed her eyes. "Why?"

"We've been needing to update our website. It would be great if you could take some pictures during a class. I bet, with your skills, you'd make the school look amazing."

"Sure, I can do that."

"Great!"

Lucy had been right. Her dinner had tasted amazing. And she had thoroughly enjoyed catching up with Lucy. Though she was stuffed from dinner when she got home, the box of cupcakes from Nick were waiting for her, and she couldn't resist opening the box. They were gorgeous cupcakes. Holly smiled as her mind was filled with the image of Nick decorating each one.

She couldn't resist. She had to have one. She chose the red one with Merry Christmas written on it with white frosting. She carefully pulled the cupcake paper away and admired the work of art before trying it. Her teeth sunk into the spongy cake, and she actually moaned at how delicious it was. It was the most delectable thing she'd ever tasted—and she'd had the best desserts in New York City to compare it to.

As she enjoyed her treat, she spotted a small note inside the box. Pulling it out, she found a hand-written note.

Dear Holly,

I hope these make you feel welcome. Silverwood is lucky to have you here.

Sweet Greetings,
Nick

Holly smiled, reading the note twice more before she put it back in the box. He'd written her a note. She wondered if he did that for everyone who got a welcome box from him. Somehow, she doubted it. A note and cupcakes. *Sweet greetings*. He made them himself, just for her. Maybe Nick wasn't so bad after all.

Chapter Ten

Holly's coffee warmed her hand as she walked into the art school and out of the cold. The coffee was from The Gingerbread House. She hadn't wanted to admit it, but she had been disappointed that Nick wasn't at the shop when she went in. She wanted to thank him again for the cupcakes and let him know how much she'd enjoyed the one she'd eaten so far. She was sure he would have enjoyed that stroke to his ego. The coffee was good though, so it hadn't been a wasted trip.

Emily waved at her, a huge smile on her face. "You're just in time. The next class is about to start."

"Great!"

Holly followed a group of kids into the classroom. They were all talking and giggling and discussing what they wanted for Christmas. Holly found a chair near the front of the room and set down her camera bag. Lucy took out some supplies as she told the class to settle down.

"Thanks for letting me sit in," Holly said to Emily.

"Of course! You're always welcome here." Emily touched her shoulder. "In fact, we were just trying to see how to juggle these schedules around once Lucy goes on maternity leave. Usually we make it work, between the two other teachers, but one is skiing with her fiancé in Colorado, and the other can only work part-time because she's taking college classes. I was wondering how long you were thinking of staying in Silverwood."

"You want me to fill in for Lucy?" Holly asked.

"Only if it doesn't interfere with your schedule. Lucy mentioned you were taking some time off to figure out your next steps. I just didn't know how much time that would be. And maybe teaching an art class for a few weeks could serve as a refreshing change. These kids," Emily gestured to the class, "they can do wonders for the soul."

Holly nodded, her mind whirring. She'd only meant to be in Silverwood for the holidays. But extending her stay a few weeks wouldn't be out of the question. She wouldn't have to rush figuring out what she wanted to do, and it wasn't like she was needed back in New York right away.

"Can I think about it?" Holly asked.

"Yes, dear. Of course. It's a lot to ask."

"Thanks. Um, Lucy also mentioned you need new pictures for the website. I brought my camera."

"That would be perfect! Holly, you're a blessing. Truly."

The classroom door opened, and Avery stepped in. Rachel was right behind her.

"Sorry we're late," Rachel said to Lucy. "I had to drop my dad off at his appointment."

"Avery's just in time," Lucy reassured her. "Don't worry about it."

"Thanks, Lucy. You're the best." Rachel stroked Avery's hair. "I'll pick you up after class."

Avery nodded and ran off to join her friends.

"Oh, hi, Holly," Rachel said to her.

"Hi, Rachel. Um, I stopped into the shop to thank Nick for the cupcakes, but he wasn't there. If you see him, could you tell him thanks for me?"

"Sure. So, you liked them?"

"I only had one so far. But it was absolute heaven. Nick really made them?"

"Yeah. It was our mom's recipe. I think it's his way of keeping her memory alive."

"That's sweet. Oh, pun intended, I guess."

Rachel noticed the class starting to settle. "I've got to run, but I'll see you soon."

"Good to see you."

They waved at each other before Rachel turned to leave.

Avery spotted Holly and skipped over to her. "I didn't know you worked here."

"Oh, I don't. I'm sitting in on your class today, though." Holly held up her camera. "And I'm going to be taking pictures."

"Cool."

Lucy clapped her hands together and faced the class. "All right, I think we're ready to begin. Today's project was Bianca's suggestion, so thank you, Bianca, for the idea. We're making Christmas tree ornaments made of sparkly yarn. And the trick is to blow up a balloon to the size of a Christmas ball. Holly, would you like to help me hand out the yarn while I get everyone a balloon?"

"Sure." Holly took the tub of sparkly yarn and made her way through the worktables. The students chose the colors they wanted while trying to blow up their balloons. Lucy and Emily ended up helping half of the students inflate their balloons, as there were only two air pumps being shared between the class. It wasn't long before the class bubbled with laughter at their efforts.

"What color yarn would you like, Avery?" Holly asked.

Avery paused trying to blow up her balloon. "Our tree is pretty colorful."

"Well, which one is your favorite?"

"Purple."

Holly handed her the yarn and whispered, "That's my favorite too."

Avery smiled up at her.

"Do you need help with your balloon?" Holly asked.

Avery tried once again, fitting the balloon's opening to her mouth and blowing. The uninflated balloon flew from her mouth and landed on the worktable. A laugh escaped from Holly's lips before she could stop it, but her laughter was soon joined by Avery's.

Holly quickly set down the tub of yarn and lifted her camera, which hung around her neck by its strap. She snapped a couple shots of Avery laughing, and then took a new balloon from her pile.

"I'll give it a try," Holly said.

The balloons were small, so it was difficult to inflate them, but the class eventually succeeded in their mission and began running their yarn through paste and wrapping the balloons with it. Everyone was a mess by the end of the class, so Lucy sent them all to wash their hands at the basins installed at the side of the classroom.

"I'll hang these to dry," Lucy announced, "and in our next class we can pop the balloons."

Emily said goodbye to all the kids as they left the classroom. Smiling at how she'd spent the last forty-five minutes, Holly packed her camera away and helped Lucy clean up.

"That was a lot of fun," Holly said.

"Making a mess is always fun." Lucy gave her a wink. "But I don't need to tell you that, Miss Papier Mâché."

They made their way out to the lobby.

"I can send you the pictures tonight," Holly told Emily. "I think I got some good ones. I also shot the outside of the school earlier."

"Sounds good."

In the lobby, Avery sat on the couch, still peeling glue from her fingers. Lucy checked her phone.

"Oh, Avery," Lucy said. "Your mom just messaged me. She's running a little late but shouldn't be too long."

"Okay." Avery smiled at her.

Holly wandered over to the couch. "How's Dasher?"

"Fine. He was trying to catch snowballs with his mouth this morning. He's so funny."

"I'd love to see that. My good friend Kim back in New York, she and I loved to get into snowball fights."

"Did you win?"

"Sometimes." Holly looked over her shoulder to see Emily and Lucy going over paperwork. She directed her attention back to

Avery. "See those paintings? Guess which one is mine."

Avery's eyes lit up as she scanned the wall of art. "Um, the one with the playground?"

"Nope."

"Hmm. The mean-looking lady holding a cactus?"

Holly laughed. "No, but you're close. It's the one next to it."

"That pretty tree?"

Holly nodded. "That's mine."

"I like it."

"I was about your age when I painted it."

"Cool. I have one up there too." Avery smirked. "Guess which one."

"The mean-looking lady with the cactus?" Holly joked.

Avery burst into giggles. "No. It's the dog sleeping under the chair."

"Oh, I should have guessed. Is that Dasher?"

"Yeah, when he was a puppy."

Holly studied the painting. She saw real potential. "It's really good."

"Thanks."

The door opened and Rachel walked in. "I'm so sorry I'm late."

"That's okay, Mommy. I was talking with Holly." Avery stood and grabbed her backpack. "Bye, Holly."

"Thanks for keeping her company, Holly," Rachel said. "You should stop by the shop tomorrow. Nick's working, and you can tell him in person how much you liked his cupcakes."

Holly felt a tingle in her chest. "Yeah, sure. Thanks."

As Rachel and Avery left, Holly grabbed her things.

"I probably should get going," she said to Emily and Lucy. "But thank you so much for letting me sit in today. It was a lot of fun."

"You can sit in any time," Lucy said. "I can't wait to see the pictures."

"We love having you here," Emily added. "You bring great energy. And please, think over what we talked about."

Holly nodded once. "I will. Thanks."

As she left the building, a strange feeling came over her. She was torn. She really did feel at home, working with Emily and Lucy. And making art with the kids was fulfilling. It wasn't as if she was leaving her old life behind forever. She would just be covering for Lucy while she was out. She really didn't see a downside to accepting Emily's offer.

It was just a shame that Emily would be handing off the place to someone else.

Chapter Eleven

Holly was admiring a music box in one of the store windows when her phone rang. Kim's name and picture popped up on the screen, making Holly smile.

"Hey, Kim. Happy holidays!"

"Whoa," Kim replied. "Do I have the right number?"

"Yeah, it's me."

"What's going on? Are you in trouble? Is *happy holidays* code for 'Rescue me. I'm being held hostage in a strange town where the people are made out of fruitcake'?"

"No. Everything is fine. I'm actually out doing some shopping. I thought I'd get some canvas and paint and see what happens."

"Oh, are you feeling inspired by mountain scenery and falling snow?"

"Something like that." Holly glanced down the street at the sign for The Gingerbread House. "I'm welcome to inspiration."

"So, you don't feel inspired to come racing back to New York and have dinner so we can gossip?"

"As much as I'd love that, I think I'm hanging out here a while longer. Besides, I don't exactly have a career to go running back to.

The other shoe finally dropped."

"Okay, that must be code for something."

Despite the sore subject, Holly let out a laugh. "My agent dumped me."

"What? When did this happen?"

"Pretty recently. But it's taken some time for me to really grasp the reality of it."

"Oh, Holly, that sucks. I'm so sorry." At least this time, Kim's whiny voice fit the situation.

Holly sighed. "It is what it is. I mean, I came here to try to reinvent myself and start all over. So I might as well start all over in that area of my not-so-perfect life too."

"Things will look up. I just know they will."

"Thanks, Kim. But, yeah, I think I'll be hunkering down here until I figure out what I'm doing with my life."

"Fine. Guess I'll be holding a gossip session over the phone, then."

Holly laughed. "Go on. Spill."

"You know Karen?"

"The colleague from hell who stole your promotion?"

"One and the same. Well, guess who just got fired for stealing from the company?"

"No! Are you serious?"

"So now Mr. Peterson wants to have a meeting with me. Friday."

Holly gasped. "You think he'll offer you her position?"

"If he doesn't, I'm walking. They need to learn to respect my hard work."

"Preach! Keep me up to date with that."

"I definitely will."

Holly moved on to the next store window. "I'm crossing my fingers for you. What else is going on?"

"Grayson was asking about you again."

Holly rolled her eyes. "Can't that man take a hint?"

"He'd need a brain to be able to do that."

"That's true. You didn't tell him where I am, did you?"

"I'd never betray you like that, Holly. I'd sooner send him on a wild goose chase to the Bermuda Triangle. He's not trying to call you again, is he?"

"I wouldn't know. I blocked him on everything. I don't need that kind of negativity in my life."

"Preach!"

As they laughed, Holly spotted an older woman walking an Alaskan Malamute coming her way. She wondered which of the siblings this dog was.

"Well, I'm going to let you get back to shopping," Kim said. "Make sure you find something nice for your old friend Kim, okay?"

"Top of my list," Holly promised. "Talk to you soon."

Her eyes were still on the dog as the woman got closer. She swore she couldn't tell any of them apart. The dogs all looked the same to her.

Holly smiled at the woman. "Excuse me. This is probably a crazy question, but I was wondering which of the famous Malamute siblings your dog might be. I've met Cupid and Dasher so far."

"Oh." The woman adjusted her hold on the leash. "Well, this is Vixen. She's one of the youngest of the bunch."

"May I?" Holly asked as she bent down toward Vixen.

"Yeah, sure."

Holly held her hand out for Vixen to smell. Vixen sniffed her and then looked Holly in the face, panting. Holly could have sworn the dog was smiling at her.

"Hi, Vixen." Holly gave her a scratch behind the ear. "Nice to meet you."

"You must know Nick, then," the woman said, "if you've met Cupid and Dasher."

"Yes." Holly stood upright again. "And Rachel and Avery. And Mr. Mason, too. I'm Holly, by the way."

"Nice to meet you, Holly. I'm Gretta." Gretta studied her. "You look like a woman I knew who used to come to Silverwood every winter. Vivian St. Ives."

"She's my mother."

Gretta's eyes widened, as did her smile. "Oh, well, would you look at that. Small world. Is she in town as well?"

"No. I'm on my own this year."

"Well, if you speak with her, you tell her Gretta says hello and Merry Christmas."

"I definitely will. Nice meeting you, Gretta. You too, Vixen."

Holly waved as they parted, and she continued down the sidewalk until she came to the art supply shop. The bell above the door chimed as she entered. It had been awhile since Holly had seen an actual bell being used. Every small shop in New York she could think of had an electronic bell instead. The next thing Holly noticed was that the shop wasn't overly stuffed with supplies like the place she frequented in the city. She found this layout more appealing because she wasn't overwhelmed with an abundance of materials she really didn't need.

With a couple small canvases in her basket, Holly moved over to the acrylic paints. A shelf of pastels caught her eye, and Holly thought of Avery. She snatched up a box of them and picked out a couple of sketch books for her as well. Maybe it was a bit premature or presumptuous to buy Avery a Christmas present, but it wasn't as if she were buying her some lavish, materialistic gift. These were art supplies. She was supporting a child's interest in something cultural.

Pleased with her purchases, she headed out to find Kim the present she promised her.

She was craving a hot chocolate by the time she reached The Gingerbread House. Forcing herself to slow her breathing, she stepped inside and ignored the acceleration of her heartbeat. She scanned the shop for Nick but found Avery and Rachel behind the counter. Rachel gave her a smile and a wave as she continued her work. As Holly got closer, she realized Avery was standing on a chair. She had her hair tied up out of her face and was holding a frosting dispenser, placing tiny sugar dots on some cupcakes.

She was about to greet her when her grandfather came out of the back room holding a tray of gingerbread cookies. Mr. Mason looked up at her and had an instant smile on his face.

"Hello, again." He almost lost his balance as he set the tray down on the counter beside Avery.

"You okay, Dad?" Rachel asked him.

"Yes, yes, I'm fine." He gave a little chuckle as he wiped his hands on his apron. "Holly, aren't you a sight for sore eyes?"

"Hello, Mr. Mason."

"Oh, no." He shook a finger at her playfully. "You can call me Nicholas."

"All right." She shifted her focus to Avery. "Hi, Avery. I didn't know you worked here."

Avery giggled. "I'm helping decorate cupcakes."

Holly propped herself up on her tiptoes and studied Avery's work. "You're really good at that."

"She is, isn't she?" Rachel asked.

"It's kind of like painting," Avery explained. "Except you can eat it."

"Edible art," Mr. Mason said with a laugh. "Avery says you're an artist. You want to try it?"

"Really?" Holly's eyes widened, and she rubbed her hands together.

"Sure," Mr. Mason said. "Come on back. I'll get you an apron."

"Do you have something to tie your hair back?" Avery asked.

Holly marveled at how insightful this eight-year-old was. "I think I do."

As Mr. Mason fetched an apron, Holly dug in her purse and found a hair band. She tied her hair up just in time to accept the apron Mr. Mason handed her. Holly slipped off her coat and used it to cover the bag of art supplies she bought. Avery grinned as she handed Holly the frosting dispenser.

"You just squeeze here," Avery said, "and press the frosting where you want it."

It took Holly a minute to figure out how to work the dispenser properly, but once she got the hang of it, she had to agree with Avery. It really was like creating art. She wanted to keep going, feeling as if she could spend hours decorating the cupcakes, but she didn't want to take the task away from Avery. She handed back the dispenser and let out a happy breath. "Thanks so much. That was fun."

"Can I get you anything?" Rachel asked. "Or did you come in for something else."

Rachel's knowing smile made Holly clear her throat.

"I, uh, just wanted to thank Nick for the gift." Holly pulled the hair band from her hair and let it fall back to her shoulders.

"He's in the back." Rachel winked. "He'll be out in a second."

"Okay, thanks."

Rachel dusted her hands off on her apron and pressed her hip against the counter. "Avery tells me you used to go to the art school when you were younger."

"Yeah." Holly nodded, still trying to fight off her nervousness. "Every year when my family would spend the holidays in Silverwood. I looked forward to it each year."

"It's a great school."

Holly's mind dwelled on the fact that Emily would be retiring and was considering having someone take over for her. But she didn't want to bring it up, just in case Emily didn't want that news to be public.

Someone stepped out of the back room, but Holly couldn't tell who it was because the person's upper body and face were blocked by an enormous, hand-crafted dollhouse. It wasn't until he spoke that Holly knew it was Nick.

"Okay, Avery, the staircase is fixed."

He set down the dollhouse on a back counter and turned to face Avery. His eyes widened and a smile crept across his face when he realized Holly was there. Holly felt a flutter in her belly at making eye contact with him, but she tried to appear as if his presence wasn't making her nervous.

"Hey, Nicky," Holly teased.

Nick wiped his brow, and his smile turned shy. "Hi, Holly. Great to see you."

Holly pointed. "That is an amazing dollhouse."

"Uncle Nick built it for me," Avery said, looking smug.

Holly's jaw practically dropped from her face. "You made this?"

He half-shrugged. "I'm somewhat of an amateur carpenter."

"My son's being modest," Mr. Mason said. "He could go pro if he wanted."

Nick kept his eyes on Holly but raised his brow. "Because, apparently, I don't have enough jobs."

Holly almost snorted with laughter.

"But, really," Rachel added, "he's good. He made our dining table."

Avery gasped. "Uncle Nick, you even fixed the skylight!" She jumped up from inspecting the dollhouse and ran over to hug Nick's waist. "Thank you so much!"

Holly couldn't hold back. She was too curious to resist checking out Nick's work. The dollhouse was a picture of perfection. The wooden boards that made up the floors were perfectly perpendicular to the walls. Each room had tasteful wallpaper that matched the area rugs. The spiral staircase looked like something out of a catalog of dream houses. This didn't look like an amateur job at all. This looked like something a top-notch professional who'd been in the business for years could have done.

It was one thing to try to be a jack-of-all-trades to feed your ego, but Holly had to admit that Nick was really talented.

"This is amazing," Holly said, still taking in the details.

"I didn't make *all* the furniture." Nick scrubbed at his beard. "Just the dining table and chairs. And the beds. The nightstands. The cupboards. Oh, and the coffee table."

"And the rocking chair," Avery added.

"Oh, yeah, right." Nick half-shrugged again.

Holly stood and gazed at Nick, shaking her head. "I have to say, there seems to be no end to all the ways you impress me. I was just telling Rachel yesterday how much I enjoyed your cupcakes."

"I'm glad you liked them." His adorable dimple appeared when he smiled.

Rachel excused herself to help a customer, and Mr. Mason brought Avery back to the counter to help her with the frosting.

Holly studied the dollhouse once more. "You know, my father was into woodwork as well."

"Oh, yeah?" Nick rested his hands on his sides.

"In fact … My dad made a sleigh that I think you'd be interested in seeing. It was his obsession project."

"That sounds great." He held her gaze. "I'd love to see it."

"Then you should come up to my cabin when you have a

chance." Her heart sped up. Did she just invite Nick to her place? She almost felt lightheaded, clearing her throat. "I'll give you the address."

"Oh, I know where it is."

"You do?"

"Yeah. You're neighbors with Mrs. Miranelli, right?"

"That's right." She swiped her hair away from her cheek.

"Maybe tomorrow?"

She ignored the flush of heat that crept up her neck and face. "Sure. Can't wait."

Chapter Twelve

Holly wasn't surprised to find it was Mrs. Miranelli who had rung her doorbell. If Holly were a paranoid person, she would have started to believe her mother had convinced Mrs. Miranelli to drop in every couple of days to check on her. But actually, Mrs. Miranelli was simply super friendly and probably seeking out someone to talk to besides her husband.

"Hi, Mrs. Miranelli." Holly held her door open.

Mrs. Miranelli held a container in her hand. "I brought cookies!"

Holly bit back a laugh. "Come in."

"I made too many," Mrs. Miranelli said as she walked inside and slipped off her snow-covered boots. "I simply got carried away and made too much cookie dough. Didn't want it all to go to waste and figured you might feel snacky all alone here in this quiet cabin."

"That's so nice of you. Thanks!"

"Oh, it's my pleasure, believe me. Henry is watching some documentary about fishing and I was about to go crazy. Felt like I was stuck in a swamp with rubber pants myself." Mrs. Miranelli chortled and playfully slapped Holly on the arm.

"Well, I'm glad I could offer a respite." She took the container of cookies and put them on the dining room table next to her open laptop.

"Oh, what's this?" Mrs. Miranelli asked, noticing the webpage Holly had open. "A real estate agent?"

"Um, yeah." Holly cleared her throat. "I was just, you know, exploring some possibilities."

Mrs. Miranelli frowned. "You're really thinking about selling?"

Holly felt cornered. "I just want to weigh my options. I haven't really decided yet."

"Oh." Mrs. Miranelli looked over the website, pursing her lips. "Well, how's it going?"

"No progress. Apparently, all the real estate agents in a hundred-mile radius of Silverwood are already on Christmas break."

Mrs. Miranelli's smile returned. "Yes, well, it's that time of year, dear."

"Seems that way."

Holly's doorbell ringing, followed by a knock on the door, made her brow furrow.

"Are you expecting company?" Mrs. Miranelli asked, craning her neck toward the door as if that would help her see who it was.

"Oh. Uh, maybe?" Holly made her way to the door, trying not to get her hopes up that it might be Nick.

Peeking through the side window, she was delighted to see Nick standing on her doorstep. She seemed to have lost her breath at the sight of him, and her mouth went dry. She ran her hands over her hair as she mentally prepared herself to open the door to greet him.

As soon as she got the door open, Cupid stood on his hind legs and waved his paw at her. She gasped in delight at the trick, placing a hand on her heart.

"Oh, wow." She looked up at Nick. "Did you teach him how to do that?"

"That would be Avery's doing," Nick answered.

"That's amazing." Holly searched for what to say next. "Um, hi! Did you want to come in?"

"If I'm not putting you out. I thought I could take a look at that sleigh."

"Of course. Come in. Both of you."

Cupid pranced inside, sniffing around. Nick kicked the snow off his boots before walking in.

"Sorry if he gets your floors wet," Nick said. His eyes darted over her face. "Should I take off my boots?"

Holly waved her hand in dismissal, hoping he didn't notice her blush. "No, don't worry about it."

They continued inside. Cupid had already made himself comfortable, curled up in front of the fireplace.

"Oh, hey, Nick," Mrs. Miranelli said. "See, Holly, even Cupid knows how great this house is."

Nick shook his head, smiling at Cupid. "He does enjoy a cozy fire. You wouldn't think so with all that fur."

"Hmm." Mrs. Miranelli glanced between Holly and Nick. "I'll just leave you two to it and get back to Henry and his fishing show. If I'm lucky he fell asleep and I can put one of my programs on."

"Good luck," Holly said. "And thanks for the cookies."

"My pleasure, dear. Bye, Nick!"

He waved as she left, and then he stuck his hands in the pockets of his jeans. "This really is a nice place. Quality workmanship. And super snug and comfy. I bet you had a blast spending your holidays here."

"Yeah, I did." Her eyes scanned the room, recalling memories past. "Lots of really solid, quality family memories."

"Funny how we missed each other all these years, since I've been living here so long, and you spent so many Christmases here. But I guess it makes sense. My mom liked the tropics. Dad liked skiing. So, they would switch it up every other year."

"That sounds nice."

"As long as I didn't accidentally pack for the wrong destination, everything was fine."

"What about their businesses?" she asked.

"They had people watching their shops while they were gone. Dad's brother took over selling the trees, but he's moved away now. Thinking back, we probably left town just as you were coming in."

"I guess we just weren't meant to meet until now." Holly averted her gaze as soon as she said it. She wondered if it truly was a matter of fate. But she couldn't assume that Nick had feelings for her. She wasn't even sure what she thought of him. Maybe her pseudo-obsession with Nick was just her mind's way of helping her forget about her disaster of a relationship with Grayson and her failed career moves. Maybe this was her way of taking a fantasy vacation from her real life.

"I guess so," he replied.

When she looked back up at him, she found him gazing at her.

She cleared her throat. "I, uh, found a picture of my parents in front of your mom's store. I mean, The Gingerbread House. Back when your mom ran it."

She retrieved the picture from the box she had set on a dining room chair. As she handed it to him, their fingers softly brushed against each other. She did her best to hide the fact that goosebumps had sprung up all over the back of her neck.

Their eyes met for a moment before he turned his attention to the picture. "I wonder if my parents knew yours. I mean, I know we were never really around at the same time. But maybe they did run into each other at some point, before you and I came along."

She shrugged. "Anything is possible."

"Where are they now?"

She tried not to make it apparent that she was taking a long breath before answering. Crossing her arms over her chest, she leaned against the back of one of her dining room chairs. "My mother is in the Philippines helping my aunt, who's not doing so well. And my father ... passed away a couple of years ago."

Nick frowned. "Oh. I'm sorry to hear that. I'm sorry for your loss."

She nodded, her eyes trained on the floor. "Thank you for saying that."

"Losing a parent isn't easy. I, uh, know how it feels."

She looked up at him but didn't say anything, waiting for him to continue.

"My mom passed away when I was in my late teens," he explained.

She remembered Rachel mentioning that Nick used her recipes to keep her memory alive. "That must have been tough on you and Rachel."

"And on my dad, of course. But yeah. I think, especially when you're young, you don't know how to deal with that kind of grief."

"I'm sorry," she said, her voice small.

"Thanks. It was a long time ago. Time heals all wounds." He offered her a small smile as he handed back the picture. "In any case, this is a great house. I can see why they bought it. Except for that mailbox out front. That doesn't seem like it's up to code."

"Yeah." She scratched under her ear. "I might be selling it, actually."

"The mailbox?"

"No, the house."

His brows came down. "Oh really? That would be a shame."

"I don't know. I might keep it. Like as a holiday house or something? I'm still trying to figure out what I'm going to do."

He nodded silently, studying her face.

She pushed her hair back and crossed her arms again. "Um, do you want to see the sleigh?"

"Yeah. I'm excited to."

"Okay, this way."

She swore she felt his eyes on her as she led the way to the garage, but then again, it was probably just in her head. In any case, she tried to ignore the tickle that played on her spine. Cupid jumped up and followed them, sniffing along as he walked. She opened the connecting door to the garage and stepped back to let Nick walk by. Cupid bounded in after him.

She'd never put the tarp back on the sleigh, so the big, red, vehicle was first and foremost in Nick's view when he entered the garage. Holly caught the sight of Nick's jaw dropping as he neared it. He was quiet at first, simply studying the sleigh. And Holly felt the silence pressing in on her.

"I've got to say," he began, "this is not what I was expecting. For some reason I had a small thing in my head, like an exaggerated sled. I didn't realize it was something as masterful as this."

Holly felt a surge of pride for her father's work. She watched as Cupid circled the sleigh, sniffing the rails.

Nick examined it, running his hands along the wood. He seemed to be inspecting every detail, as if he was checking it for quality. Or as if he was figuring out in his head how her father had made it. At long last, he turned to Holly.

"This sleigh is amazing," he said. "I mean, really. It's a masterpiece."

Holly gave him a half-shrug, smiling from ear to ear. "Yeah, Dad was pretty proud of it."

Nick stood back to admire it. "What is this, fifteen feet?"

"I don't know. I guess. Like the length of a car, right?"

Nick rubbed his jaw. "Might be a bit more. Wow. That's quite a project."

"It did take him years to complete. It was his winter obsession."

"You think he got the wood in Silverwood?"

"I'm willing to bet he did."

Nick moved around the back. "What's this lever?"

Something clicked, and the back part of the sleigh folded down, extending the bed.

"Dad wanted to have a section that popped out in the back in case Santa had an extra big load." Holly came over to join Nick.

He backed up at the same time, bumping into her. Swiftly, he turned and took her arm. "I'm sorry. Don't want to knock you over."

His hand was still on her arm as she looked up at him. Her knees felt weak and her breathing felt restricted.

"No problem," she said softly. "I'm fine."

"It's, uh, convenient," he said.

"What?"

He turned toward the sleigh. "The extension in the back. If you wanted to fill it or have extra passengers. It's like the sleigh version of an SUV or a van."

"I think he imagined filling it with half the town for sleigh rides."

Nick moved to the front of the sleigh and stepped up to the coach area. He whistled as he ran his hand along the bench cushion. "Your dad didn't spare any expense, did he? This is quality material."

"When he did something, he wanted to do it right."

Nick flashed her a smile.

She almost swooned at the sight of him. The word *handsome* didn't even cover it. Add to that his charm and determination and sense of responsibility, and any woman would be putty in his capable hands.

She averted her eyes, realizing she was staring at his hands.

"How much do you want for it?" he asked.

"Oh." Holly crossed her arms and shook her head. "Oh no. I

couldn't take money for it. That's not why my dad made it. I want to donate it to the Christmas festival."

He smiled at her. "Really?"

"I'm totally serious."

"I don't know what to say."

"Say that you'll pick it up so I don't have to deliver it to you." She tilted her head and gave him a snarky smile.

He laughed. "Just when I thought your Christmas spirit might be taking over."

"Maybe I'm just on a sugar high from those delicious cupcakes."

He let out a small laugh, averting his eyes. Was he blushing?

"It'll fit just fine in my truck bed, no problem." He pulled out his phone. "I'll have to check my schedule to see when I can pick it up."

They headed back inside the house with Cupid running up behind them.

"Sure, let me know." She stopped once they were well in the house and turned to him. "Give me your phone, I'll put in my number."

"Okay." He handed her his phone.

She pretended not to notice that their fingers touched again. She typed in her information, feeling him watching her. As she handed it back, she caught his eyes on her. But he looked down at his phone almost as soon as their eyes met. She released his phone and stuffed her hands in the back pockets of her jeans. If only the fluttering in her stomach would stop, she might be able to act normal.

He lifted his chin and looked around the cabin. "That's a nice painting," he suddenly said.

Holly followed his gaze to the painting above the fireplace.

"Oh, thanks." She wrapped her arms around herself. "That's one of mine."

He turned his focus back to her. "Really?"

"Yeah, I'm uh, somewhat of an artist."

"That's right. Mrs. Miranelli mentioned you're a big shot in the New York art scene."

"Well, I wouldn't say 'big shot.' Not anymore anyway."

"Oh yeah?" He scratched his lip with his teeth. "What happened?"

The second she opened her mouth to answer, she snapped it shut again. She wasn't ready to spill her sad sob story of failure to Nick quite yet. "Let's call it a hiccup in my career. That's sort of why I'm here. I'm waiting to be inspired again."

He narrowed his eyes, obviously skeptical about her answer. "Okay. Hiccups happen. I'm sure you'll figure out something that inspires you. You never know. Sometimes it's right in front of you, but you've got to take a second to realize it's there."

Was he flirting with her? Her gaze dropped to the floor.

He was quiet for a moment, and then he shifted his stance. "No tree?" he asked.

"What?"

He smirked, stuffing his phone in his pocket. "You're here for Christmas but you don't have a tree."

"What?" It took her a second to focus on what he was saying. "Oh. No. I don't, um, have one."

"New Yorkers don't believe in Christmas trees? Don't you guys usually have a big one at Rockefeller Center?"

"Oh, I probably won't put one up." She waved a hand. "It's a lot of hassle when I'm just going to have to take it down before I head back."

He gave her a sideways smile, a cute dimple appearing in his cheek. "Come on. Maybe if you put a tree up, you can let a little more of that Christmas spirit back in your life. Or are you so set in your cold, big city ways that you don't believe in Christmas anymore?"

"No, it's not that. It's just … I'll see if I can fit it into my schedule."

"Busy New Yorker, huh?" His eyes roamed her face. "Well, maybe Santa will send some Christmas elves to help you out."

Before she could answer, he gave her a nod and walked toward the door.

"Come on, Cupid. Time to go." He pulled the door open and smiled at Holly. Cupid darted outside. "Thanks again for the sleigh. Really. It's gonna make a big hit at the festival."

As the door closed behind him, Holly had mixed feelings. What was it to her if Nick thought she wasn't into Christmas? Was it really that important? She'd been generous in donating the sleigh. What more did he want from her? And had he been flirting with her? If so, why did she feel like he'd been judging her? Holly raked her fingers through her hair, totally confused by Nick's words and actions. With a pout, she opened Mrs. Miranelli's container of cookies and stuffed one in her mouth.

Chapter Thirteen

Holly studied her computer screen, perusing the pictures she'd taken in town. There were lots to choose from, but she wanted to find the one that would get her back into her groove. She wanted her muse to call out to her. But she just wasn't finding it. These pictures were not exciting her. There was nothing artistic about any of the shots. She sighed and closed her laptop.

Her stomach grumbled for the tenth time that hour, and Holly grimaced at the dull ache that was growing into an intolerable pain. When she suddenly doubled over because of the intense cramp in her stomach, she knew she had to do something about it. After searching through her things and futilely checking the medicine cabinets, she resolved to making a trip to the drug store to get something that would help.

"Oh, man, Mrs. Miranelli," Holly mumbled through clenched teeth. "What did you put in those cookies?"

She normally wasn't one to go out to a shop in her sweat clothes, but this was an emergency. And no one would really pay any attention to her anyway, would they? She slipped her snow boots on and climbed into her car. As she drove, she distracted herself by admiring how the stars shining over the town created a beautiful backdrop against the mountaintops.

She breathed through her pain, telling her stomach to shut up when it gurgled at her for attention. She didn't think it was bad enough to go to the emergency room. Praying it was just some bad acid from something she ate, she followed her navigation system to the drug store, glad to find it was still open. She waited until her ache wasn't causing her to bend over from the intensity, and then made her way to the store's entrance.

Outside of the drugstore, sitting near a bench in the front with a leash secured to it, was an Alaskan Malamute. Grateful for the distraction, she wondered if it was Cupid or one of the other dogs she'd met. If it was Cupid, that might mean Nick was in the store. Though, did she really want him seeing her like this?

Approaching the dog cautiously, Holly studied the Malamute. The dog studied her too, standing up and sniffing at the air around her. He looked friendly. Holly glanced through the store window to see if anyone was watching her.

"Hey, buddy." She crouched down to pet it. "I'm not feeling too well, but somehow you've taken my mind off my pain a bit."

She reached around its neck and read the tag on his collar.

"Donner." She nodded. "Nice to meet you. I'm Holly. It seems I'm making the rounds and meeting your whole family."

With one final scratch behind his ear, she stood and made her way into the store.

Glad that the aisles were clearly labeled, Holly grabbed a bottle of antacids and some liquid upset-stomach medicine and slipped them into her shopping basket. She quickly grabbed a few more things she might need, like bandages and aspirin.

As she walked through the next aisle, she heard someone say, "Mr. Mason."

Mr. Mason?

Holly wondered if the person might be addressing Nick. She grinned at the prospect as she rounded the corner of the aisle. Her knees felt weak, but she wasn't sure if it was because Nick might be in the shop or because her stomach cramps were getting the better of her.

She swiped the loose hair from her ponytail out of her face, mumbling a curse when she realized she was in sweat clothes. Plus, she was probably pale and sweaty from fighting off her stomachache. Not her best look.

When she found it was Nick's father and not Nick, she let out a quiet laugh at how foolish she'd been acting.

The pharmacist—a young, olive-skinned woman with her hair tied in a bun—handed Mr. Mason a bottle of pills. The bottle slipped from his hands, and he looked as if he were having a hard time picking them up.

"You all right, Mr. Mason?" the pharmacist asked.

Mr. Mason stood upright, his hands slightly shaking as he gripped the pill bottle. "Yes, dear. I'm fine."

"All right. Don't forget to call Doctor Leptenstein if you have any side effects, like nausea or loss of appetite," the pharmacist said.

"I will, dear."

"That refill should last you another month." She handed him his receipt. "We're all rooting for you, Mr. Mason."

He gave the woman a nod. "Thanks, Jean."

As he backed away from the counter, Holly jerked back and accidentally knocked a box off a shelf, which caused Mr. Mason and the pharmacist to look her way. Sheepishly, Holly waved at Mr. Mason and bent down to retrieve the fallen box.

"Holly, hello." Mr. Mason cleared his throat as his fist closed around the bottle of pills. He approached her with a bit of a hop in his step, and he began singing a line from *Holly, Jolly Christmas*. He stopped when he noticed the container of antacids and medicine for upset stomachs in Holly's basket. "Oh, not so jolly at the moment, I take it."

"Not exactly."

"Sorry about that. Happens to the best of us, unfortunately." He quickly glanced down at his closed fist.

"Sorry for overhearing your conversation." She glanced at the pharmacist, who was busy typing something into her computer. "I don't want to pry."

He let out a sigh. "No, no. It's perfectly, uh, fine. Practically the whole town knows anyway."

A crease formed between Holly's brows.

Mr. Mason fidgeted with the hem of his pocket. "I have Wilson's disease."

She scrunched up her brow some more. "I don't think I've ever heard of that."

"It's a genetic disorder that inhibits my ability to process copper. Without the proper treatment, I could damage my liver, my heart, my kidneys, and eventually … well, you get the picture."

"Oh, I'm so sorry." She tried to process the information, sad that someone so nice was sick. She felt like hugging him but restrained herself. "Is there a cure?"

"Nope. No cure."

"Oh, no. But you've got medication, so it's manageable, right?"

"Well, I'm not one to complain, but these big, fancy, pharmaceutical corporations think the average man is made of money, so my pills run me about ten grand a year."

Holly's eyes widened. "What? That's insane!"

"Tell me about it. So, it's a little hard to manage, in that respect." He seemed worried that others might have overheard him. He glanced around, but the shop wasn't very full. "But don't worry yourself. I'll be fine."

She didn't want to intrude any more on his personal life, so she gestured toward the register. "I'm going to check out my purchases."

"I'll walk you out," he offered with a smile.

"Sure." Her heart warmed. "How nice of you."

As the cashier rang her up, Holly glanced at Mr. Mason. It hurt her heart that he was in this predicament. He was such a kind man, always smiling and full of cheer. Not to mention the spitting image of Santa Claus. She wondered why Nick hadn't mentioned anything to her about his father's illness. It certainly explained his hard-core work ethic. No wonder he was on a million committees and working three full-time jobs. Her whole perception of Nick completely changed. His ego wasn't the reason he worked so hard. It was his family.

After she bought her necessities, she and Mr. Mason stepped out into the cold. Donner was gone, and she thought it was a shame she hadn't met his owner. Something told her that she'd run into him again one day. It was bound to happen sooner or later.

"Do you need a ride home, Mr. Mason?"

"Call me Nicholas, dear. And, no I've got my car." He pointed to a light blue 1960s Pontiac GTO parked a row apart from Holly's car.

"That's your car?" Holly couldn't help but walk toward it. She whistled. "Wow, a classic."

"You like it?"

"Yeah, they don't make them like this anymore." She ran her hand over the cold hood. It wasn't in mint condition, but it was still pretty impressive. "My dad had an old Mustang. He loved that car. I can still remember us taking drives in it when I was a kid."

"Sounds fantastic." He took out his keys.

"Well, I better let you go." She held up her shopping bag. "I need to nurse myself back to normal."

"Feel better, dear. And I'll see you at the tree lighting ceremony."

"Right. Okay. Goodnight."

Again, she felt the urge to hug him. To tell him everything was going to be okay. But she resisted. She left him with a wave. As she walked back to her car, she realized her stomach already felt a little better. She supposed there was good medicine in having nice company.

Chapter Fourteen

Holly wiped the white silicone off her hands as she walked around the room and checked the art students' progress.

"We're going for one-eighth of an inch in thickness," Holly said. "This will give us enough depth to press in our tiles and jewels and beads, so they don't fall off."

"Like this?" one of the students asked.

"Yes, that's it." Holly smiled at her. "Great work."

"This is hard," another student said, struggling to squeeze her silicone out of her tube.

Holly went over to give the young girl a hand. "This is the hardest part of making the wreathes. Once we've got a good layer of silicone on our wooden circles, the rest is easy and completely up to your imagination."

She glanced over at Avery, who had already spread out her silicone with the putty knife. The small wooden wreath base was evenly covered and ready to be dressed up.

"Once you've got your silicone set," Holly said, "you're going to want to place your bigger feature items on the wreath so they don't all end up in the same spot—unless that's the look you're going for."

She walked over to Avery's worktable and admired her placement of shiny, patterned, broken china. "Gorgeous," Holly told her.

"Thanks, Holly," Avery whispered back to her.

Some of the kids began chatting, others snickered as they got silicone all over their fingers. Lucy, who sat in the corner observing, gave her a thumbs-up.

The class carried on, adding their various colored flattened jewels, some beads, and glittery pearls to their mini mosaic wreathes. Some of them bragged that they were giving theirs away as a Christmas present. Others insisted they were keeping them for themselves. Avery wanted to make a second one for her grandfather.

"We'll need to set these on the workbench to dry," Holly said. "And Lucy will help you all next time to attach the hangers on the back."

Once class was almost over, Lucy instructed the class to wash up and clear their workspaces.

Avery skipped over to Holly and hugged her around her waist. "Thanks, Holly. Don't forget about the tree-lighting ceremony."

"I'll see you there," Holly answered.

"Looks like you've got a fan," Lucy said once Avery left the room.

"She's kind of grown on me too." Holly recapped the remaining tubes of silicone and placed them in a drawer.

"I'm sure it has nothing to do with who her uncle is."

The smirk Lucy gave her caused Holly to playfully swat at her.

As they made their way to the lobby, Holly noticed Emily speaking to someone in her office. The door was closed, so she couldn't hear them, but, through the glass window between the office and the lobby, Holly could see by the expression on Emily's face the conversation was a serious one.

"What's going on in there?" Holly asked Lucy in hushed tones.

"I think it's someone interested in taking over the school."

"Oh, really?" Holly scrutinized Emily's face through the glass to see how the meeting was going, but she couldn't tell. "That could be promising."

"We'll see." Lucy marked some paperwork at the front desk. "I don't think she's decided what she wants to do yet. She's been bouncing around ideas. All I know is she would like to retire sometime next year, but she loves this school. So, let's see what happens."

Holly nodded and hung her purse over her shoulder.

"Hey." Lucy smiled at her. "Thanks so much for teaching today."

"Of course! It was really fun. And I think the class had a blast too."

"They definitely did." Lucy's expression changed suddenly. She hissed through her teeth and put a hand on her belly."

"What is it? Are you all right?" Holly gasped. "Oh, no! Are you going into labor?"

"No, no." Lucy blew out a long breath and set a hand on Holly's shoulder. "This happens sometimes. Probably just Braxton Hicks. Or that breakfast burrito I had this morning."

"Are you sure?"

Lucy laughed. "Yeah. See, I'm already feeling better. No panic, mechanic."

Holly placed a hand on her heart. "Thank goodness. I was drawing a blank on what to do. A voice in my head was screaming, 'Boil some water!'"

"Well, at least I'm not boring you," Lucy kidded. "Oh, that reminds me. There's an awesome churro stand at the Christmas festival. Let's meet there tomorrow before the tree lighting ceremony."

"Oh, yum! Okay, I'm in. See you there."

A blast of cold air hit her as she left the building. Wrapping her scarf around her neck, she winced against the chilly wind and headed for her car. Before she could get her keys out of her purse, she heard her ring tone chirp.

The next three seconds happened so fast, she could barely register what had happened. It wasn't until she had already accepted the call that she realized who was calling her. She'd seen the name 'Felix' on her screen, but she knew it wasn't Felix who was trying to reach her. It had to be Grayson, using his best friend's phone to throw her off. Her jaw clenched and her mind spun. She wasn't sure what to do.

"Hello?" she said, still hoping it was actually Felix and not her ex.

"Holly! Don't hang up."

She cringed at the sound of his voice. "What do you want, Grayson?"

"I just want to talk," he said, trying to sound reasonable. "Which has been nearly impossible since you blocked me on everything."

"You blocked me first."

"What? No, I didn't."

Holly scoffed. "You know what? It doesn't even matter."

"Holly, come on. Why are you shutting me out? Where are you? And why won't anyone tell me where you've gone?"

"Grayson, we're broken up. And I'm pretty sure the fight we had made it clear that we have nothing in common and shouldn't even be friends. So, it's none of your business where I am. Not now. Not ever."

He was quiet for a moment. Holly nearly hung up.

"Baby," he finally said.

"No, Grayson. You don't get to call me that. I'm not your baby. I'm not your anything."

"But you are. You mean so much to me."

Holly paced in the snow next to her car. She felt like punching something. "Oh, I see. Now I mean so much to you. Not when we were two years into a supposedly committed relationship and your social media status was still marked as 'single.' Or when you would introduce me to your colleagues as 'your friend.' Or when you would untag yourself from pictures of the two of us I would post and delete my comments on your posts and blame it on mysterious website glitches. Or when you backed out of our non-refundable trip to the Bahamas last minute so you could go on a fishing trip with your friends."

She was fuming. She felt like a dragon with all the steam coming out of her mouth and into the frosty air. She swore she'd be able to melt something if she stared at it hard enough.

"Holly, honey. Those were all just misunderstandings. Why don't you concentrate on our good times? We had a lot of fun memories. You have to admit."

"Our relationship was toxic, Grayson. *You* are toxic."

"Wait. You're putting all the blame on me?" He scoffed. "You think you can manipulate me into thinking it was my fault we broke up?"

"I'm not the manipulator here," Holly said through clenched teeth. "Don't you dare think of gaslighting me."

"Whatever, Holly. Say what you will and believe whatever you want. The truth is I'm the best thing that ever happened to you. The best! You were lucky to have even had a chance with me. You know we're bound to meet up again when you come back from wherever you are. And when we do, you won't be able to resist getting back together with me."

He hung up before she could respond. She wanted to scream, but just then the woman who'd been interviewing with Emily exited the school. Holly reached into her purse and rummaged for her keys, still fuming about Grayson. She got in her car and slammed the door, wishing there were a sure-fire way to cut him out of her life for good.

Chapter Fifteen

Holly had tossed and turned all night. This was the first night in Silverwood that she hadn't slept well. And it was all Grayson's fault. She couldn't get his dumb voice out of her head. Her mind kept replaying their conversation, and in her head, she'd come up with a hundred different ways in which she should have answered his every remark. Things that might have shut him up for good. But because she hadn't had those retorts at the time, her mind would not shut off.

At six-thirty in the morning, she grunted and resolved to get up. She needed to clear her mind. She needed to bury Grayson's voice and banish all thoughts of him from her head. She rummaged through her things and found some clothes to go hiking in. A nice walk in the brisk air should at least help her to get some mental clarity.

She made sure to dress in layers, including her socks. She packed a backpack of small snacks, water, and a first aid kit. The last item she grabbed was her camera, fully charged and ready to shoot.

The sun was just coming up, casting a faint blue light against the silhouettes of houses and trees. Holly took slow, deep breaths and told herself to clear her mind.

Movement from down the road caught her eye, and she realized it was Mrs. Miranelli. Her quirky neighbor wore an open winter coat over her robe and pajamas, her thick boots deep in the snow as she trampled around and straightened the large Christmas decorations on her lawn.

"Hi, Mrs. Miranelli." Holly waved as she approached.

"Oh hello, Holly. Where are you off to?"

"I'm a little restless so I thought I'd go for a little hike. My parents used to take me for walks on a path through the woods every time we were up here. Do you know if that path still exists?"

"It sure does." Mrs. Miranelli pulled her coat tighter around herself. "One thing you can count on about Silverwood is consistency. Not that things don't evolve around here. We try to keep up with the times. But Silverwood always grounds you in the familiar, if you ask me."

"That's comforting."

Mrs. Miranelli came closer and pointed up the road. "It's just that way about two miles up and you'll see the path on your right."

"Great, thanks." Holly glanced around the yard. "What happened here?"

"Oh, there's a loose section of my fence the deer get through now and again. I guess my reindeer garden prop looks too realistic for them to resist. Maybe they think it's a relative."

"Oh. Deer." Holly fidgeted with her camera. "Shame I missed that. I would have loved to get some pictures."

Mrs. Miranelli chortled. "Well, you won't have to wait too

long, I'm sure. I've been reminding Henry to fix that fence for years now and he hasn't gotten to it yet, so I suspect we're due another visit soon enough. Or you might see some on your walk."

"I'll keep an eye out."

"Well, I don't want to keep you. You be careful on your hike, now. You hear?"

"I will, Mrs. Miranelli." She patted her pocket. "And I've got my phone with me, just in case. Thanks."

As she set off, she thought about turning off her phone. She really didn't want to hear from Grayson again. The nerve of him. She decided to put it on silent and forget it was in her coat pocket for now. She'd already blocked Felix's number, but she was sure Grayson would simply find another friend's phone to use to break through her barrier of silence.

She spotted the beginning of the path rather easily, even though the ground was completely covered in snow. The break in the trees was wide enough to give the location away. If anything, stomping through the snowdrifts was a good workout, and she could release any aggression she had over Grayson and his stupid comments.

The white of the snow was bright against the trees, and the faint smell of pine floated in the woods. She travelled the familiar path until she came to a small brook. It was still babbling over dark rocks and pebbles. It wasn't frozen over, but judging from the ice gathered at the edges, Holly knew it would be freezing cold. She propped up her camera and crouched down, shooting the flowing water from different angles.

Silence wrapped around her like a peaceful blanket, and she

stood feeling far away from her problems. She took deep breaths and glanced upward at the bare treetops. She heard the call of a Northern Shrike and immediately lifted her camera to capture it. She was lucky that it remained perched on its branch for a few minutes before it flew off so she could get some good pictures.

She continued on, recalling the long walks she went on with her parents. She remembered how her mother was always worried that Holly wasn't warm enough, and how she would try to cut the trip short by promising everyone hot chocolate with extra marshmallows.

The peaceful hike was doing her wonders. Her problems seemed so small. She walked a good half hour in total silence, taking in the sights, smells, and small, peaceful forest sounds.

As she rounded a giant cedar, she heard a scuffling in front of her. She froze, and suddenly Lucy's voice was in her head. Bears, she had said. Holly's throat went dry and her pulse sped up. She'd never encountered a bear on any of her walks with her parents, but perhaps they had migrated closer to Silverwood since she'd been away. Swallowing hard, she scanned the trees and the snow. Should she run? Should she wait silently and try not to make a noise?

A rustling of dried leaves caused her to turn her head, and from behind a log, came a fox. Holly let out a sigh of relief and relaxed her fingers, which she realized were clamped tight around her camera strap. With her heartbeat slowing down, she was able to get her wits about her and snap some pictures of the fox before it spotted her and raced away.

Her hike got steeper as she followed the path uphill. After a while, she reached a clearing with an old, abandoned fire lookout standing before her. She captured the old structure, and then her stomach growled. She'd only had a coffee before she had set out. She was actually glad to feel the grumble of her stomach, because it meant she was getting over being upset. She could never eat when she was angry, and she hated that Grayson had that effect on her. Hunger was good. Though she had packed some small snacks in her backpack, she was craving something hot to fill her belly.

She took one more look at her surroundings and then turned to head back home.

She'd been deep in thought during her return, deciding what she might want to paint. She needed to start somewhere, just get back into the swing of it. She knew if she simply picked up a paintbrush, some inspiration would come to her.

When she reached her street, she noticed a truck outside her house.

It was a familiar truck, and she felt a little giddy inside when she realized it belonged to Nick.

She went around the truck to see him standing at the back, faced away from her and checking his phone. He stood tall, and his broad shoulders filled out his coat well. The wind played with his hair, and it looked like he'd given his beard a neat trim. Now, she wasn't sure if the funny feeling in her stomach was from hunger or from finding Nick in front of her house.

"Hey," she called out.

He turned to her and smiled. "Hi. I, uh, I tried to call you." He held up his phone.

"Oh. Sorry." She adjusted her wooly hat. "My phone was on silent, and I guess I couldn't feel it vibrate through my thick pockets."

"No problem."

Cupid ran up to her, stopped, and lifted onto his hind legs before dropping back to all fours.

Holly bent down and stroked his head. "Hey, Cupid. Nice to see you too."

Nick patted his truck. "I hope now's a good time to pick up the sleigh."

"Sure. Come on in." She headed toward her door.

He pulled down the back latch of his truck. "I also brought you a thank you."

"What?"

He pulled on some netting. Holly realized he was unloading a tree from his truck.

"Nick." She shook her head, smiling.

He gave her a wink as he slung a duffle bag over his shoulder and then hauled the tree off the truck, dragging it to her front door.

She took out her keys and unlocked the door. "You didn't have to do this."

"Yes, I did. You're missing one, and we're almost sold out, so I didn't want you to be without one. Wouldn't feel like Christmas without a tree, don't you think?"

She smiled and shrugged. "Okay, thanks. Come on in."

She kicked the snow off her boots and led him inside. Cupid ran past them both and sat by the fireplace.

"I think he wants a fire," Nick said.

"He and I both." Holly pulled her coat off and offered to take Nick's. "I ran into a couple of Cupid's siblings in town."

"You did?" Nick pulled the net off the tree. Pine needles scattered everywhere.

"Yeah, I met Vixen and Donner." She placed some logs and kindling on the fire. "So that makes four out of the nine."

"You're almost halfway there." He pulled a tree stand out of the duffle bag he'd brought in.

"You came prepared," Holly noted.

"It's not my first rodeo."

"I, uh, also ran into your dad. At the drugstore. When he was at the pharmacy."

His eyes met hers briefly before focusing back on erecting the tree. "Mm-hm."

Holly blinked. Why was he being so secretive. Mr. Mason even mentioned that the whole town knew about his illness, so why was Nick avoiding talking about it. Maybe she and Nick weren't as close as she thought. Maybe she was wrong about how he felt about her and didn't want to include her in his worries or problems. Or maybe she was just expecting too much. Clearing her throat, Holly decided to steer the conversation in another direction.

"I think my neighbor poisoned me."

Nick blinked at her. "What?"

"Yeah, it's the reason I went to the drug store. Do you remember the other day when Mrs. Miranelli was here?"

"Sure."

"Well she brought over a container of cookies."

He smirked. "Uh-oh."

"Yeah, uh-oh is right. I don't know what she put in them, but my stomach was not very happy that evening."

He appeared to be biting back a laugh. "I'm glad she didn't offer me any, then. Are you okay?"

"Yeah, all better now. It's amazing what crisp, cool air and a good dose of antacids will do for you."

He stared at her. She smiled. There was something about the way he looked at her that made her feel at peace.

His phone dinged. He took it out and glanced at the screen. "Looks like I'm needed at the festival."

"Oh." She cleared her throat to hide the disappointment in her voice. "You want to come back another time for the sleigh?"

"I think I have enough time to load it. I've got an electric dolly—sort of like a mini forklift—and the back of the truck lowers, so I'll get it in the truck bed in a matter of minutes."

"Do you need any help?" She stood up, behind her the fire slowly coming to life.

Cupid curled into a ball on the hearth.

"No, it's fine. I won't even break a sweat. You relax in here with Cupid. He looks like he wants to hang out for a bit."

"All right."

Nick gave her a nod, grabbed his coat, and went into the garage. Holly made her way to the kitchen. She was still hungry, but she also wanted to put on some coffee. As it brewed, she admired the tree Nick had set up. How thoughtful of him, she thought.

When she turned to check on Cupid, she found him on his back with his front legs bent in the air. She might have imagined it, but it looked as if he was smiling.

"Comfortable?" she asked him.

Cupid panted in response.

"So, just between you and me … Does Nick talk about me?" She squeezed her eyes shut, finding it absurd that she was talking to a dog. "You know, I used to think he was kind of egotistical and full of himself. Turns out things aren't always as they seem."

Cupid rolled on his side and lifted his head. Was that a wink she saw?

She smiled. "Our secret. I won't tell, don't worry."

The coffee finished brewing, and she'd just poured two cups when Nick came back in.

"Everything go smoothly?" she asked. She held out a coffee cup to him and smiled when he took it. She felt a little guilty for giving him reasons to stay when she knew he had somewhere he needed to be, but she decided to allow herself to be a little greedy with his time.

"Yeah, all set," he said.

"I thought you could use a little caffeine." She watched him over the rim of her cup as she took a sip.

"Thanks."

For a moment they were quiet, just sipping their coffee and stealing glances at each other.

"So, you were on a hike?"

"Yeah." She decided not to tell him that her conversation with Grayson was what triggered her need to get some mental clarity. "I was searching for some inspiration. I seem to be stuck with my creativity, and I guess I was hoping to find my muse out there."

His eyes flitted around her face. "I'm sure you'll find it. Or it'll find you."

"I hope so."

He finished his coffee. "I need to go, but thank you so much for the sleigh. And the coffee."

She took his cup. "I can't wait to see it at the festival. The sleigh, I mean."

"Let's go, Cupid." He turned back to Holly. "You decorate that tree, you hear?" He smirked at her. "I'm sure your parents left a box of ornaments around here."

"I'm positive they did. Thanks, I will."

"And keep the base watered."

"Yes, sir," she teased.

"Promise?" His eyes were intensely locked with hers.

She could only manage a whisper. "I promise."

"See you tonight at the tree lighting ceremony."

"I'll be there."

"Oh, and maybe get that mailbox fixed?" He winked before he turned toward his truck.

When she closed the door behind him, she leaned against it, holding both coffee cups to her chest and smiling.

Chapter Sixteen

The sky was streaked with tinges of pink and purple as the sun set behind the mountains. The sound of laughter and Christmas music filled Holly's ears as she approached the festival. Bright fairy lights marked each stand, and delicious scents wafted through the air. In the center of the square, the unlit Christmas tree stood, tall and regal, waiting for its audience. A small stage had been constructed beside the tree, decorated with evergreen garland and big, red ribbons.

She was a little early, so she headed to The Gingerbread House's stand to get a hot chocolate. It wasn't as cold here in the town square, so she removed her hat and stuck it in her coat pocket.

Holly could feel her face light up when she spotted Rachel at the counter. "Hi, Rachel."

"Holly! You made it."

"Everyone's going on about this tree lighting. I felt like I'd be committing a crime if I missed it."

"Yeah, I think that's how it actually works," Rachel said with a laugh.

"Is, uh, Nick here yet?" Holly tried not to make it obvious that he was the main reason she was at the festival, but she knew she wasn't fooling Rachel.

"He'll be here soon." Rachel gave her a knowing smile. "Did he bring you the tree?"

"Yes. It's really nice. He didn't have to do that."

"It's not even close enough of a thank you for donating that gorgeous sleigh. I can't believe your father made that. It's incredible!"

"Thanks." Holly scanned the area. "Is it here?"

"I think it's still on his truck. He hasn't had a chance to unload it yet, with his schedule. Plus, I think they're doing something special with the placement. Setting it near the tree in hopes it'll add some bonus points when the judges come for the tree decorating contest."

"Oh, yeah. That's a great idea."

"And the snow in the square melts too fast. They don't want the rails rusting on the wet cement, so word is they're looking for a red carpet."

"Sounds fancy. I can't wait to see it."

"Hey," Lucy said, tapping her on the shoulder. "I thought we were meeting at the churro stand."

"Lucy, hi!" Holly tucked a strand of hair behind her ear. "I was heading there after this."

Lucy leaned closer and whispered, "I'm just teasing you. I know why you're here."

"Um, hot chocolate … is why I'm here."

Lucy narrowed her eyes. "Right."

Holly turned to Rachel. "Two hot chocolates, please."

"You got it," Rachel replied. "Hey Lucy. How's it going?"

Lucy's hand automatically went to her belly. "Hanging in there, thanks."

"How long now?" Rachel asked as she handed them their order.

"She's supposed to be a New Year's baby, but the way she's kicking, I feel like she wants to come out and join the fun already."

"Can't blame her," Rachel said. "Enjoy the festivities."

"Thanks." Lucy took a quick sip, getting whipped cream all over her lip. "Let's go get those churros while they're hot."

They reached the stand and got their piping-hot churros, and Holly let the Christmas music lull her into a less stressed state of mind. Something nudged Holly's calf. She turned to find Cupid—or one of his siblings, she couldn't be sure—sniffing her boots.

"Oh." Lucy took a bite of her churro. "Hi, Cupid."

"How do you know it's Cupid?" Holly asked.

"Because here comes Nick."

Holly looked up to see Nick approaching. She waved at him with her churro, and then dropped her hand realizing how strange it must have looked. "Hi, Nick."

"Hey, Holly. Lucy. Glad you made it."

"Wouldn't miss it," Holly said.

"We're about to light the tree. You two should come closer."

"Ooh, exciting," Lucy said.

"Okay, cool." Nick gave them a nod. "Stick around afterward, okay? Holly, don't leave before I talk to you."

"What? Wait." Holly shook her head. "Where are you going?"

Nick started to back away, a smile playing on his lips. "I've just got to do a thing." He pointed over his shoulder. "You'll see in a second."

Holly turned to Lucy.

Lucy held a hand up and smirked. "Wait for it."

They moved closer to the tree. A small brass band played *We Wish You A Merry Christmas* as Nick, Mr. Mason, and Avery mounted the small stage in the square center. They were joined by a woman wearing an open, beige, winter coat with a fur-lined hood over a pantsuit. Her hair didn't move in the wind.

"Who's that?" Holly asked.

"That's Mayor McGuire," Lucy explained. "She introduces the tree lighting ceremony every year."

As the band ended the song, Mayor McGuire smiled and held her hands in the air. She stepped up to the podium that held a microphone, and the crowd applauded in greeting.

"Good evening, Silverwood!"

The crowd clapped harder.

Mayor McGuire laughed, her breath loud in the microphone. She waved her hands until the crowd calmed down, and then she patted her hair. "Thank you. Thank you. We welcome each and every one of you to Silverwood's annual Christmas Tree Lighting Ceremony. We're here to celebrate the season of hope, love, joy, and peace. This is the season of new beginnings, of miracles, and a time for giving to each other as well as forgiving one another. Silverwood has always been a special place where families and friends reach out and embrace the community with the heart of Christmas."

The crowd applauded again, which for some reason made Holly giggle.

"Keeping in mind that giving spirit, I am proud to bestow the honor of lighting the tree unto a cherished member of the Silverwood community. I don't think there's a single person in town who isn't aware of Nick Mason and the many ways he has contributed to the well-being of our fair Silverwood. So, let's hear it for this year's tree-lighter—Nick Mason, joined by his father Nicholas and niece Avery."

Holly felt a chill wash over her that made her want to applaud loudly for Nick. As the crowd began clapping and cheering, Nick stepped forward, waving his hand in the air. Cupid sidled up beside him, looking a bit bewildered at the noise, and began howling.

The next thing Holly knew, Cupid was joined by another Alaskan Malamute who ran up on stage and howled alongside him. Holly assumed it was Dasher. Laughter floated through the crowd. And … was that more howling? Holly gasped when two more of Cupid's siblings bounded onto the stage and joined in the chorus of howls. Holly couldn't help but wonder if these two were Donner and Vixen or ones she hadn't met yet.

"Oh boy," Lucy said, wincing. "Here we go."

"What?" Holly looked around. "What's happening?"

In a matter of minutes, the other five Malamutes raced on stage, one by one, and threw their heads in the air, howling along with the rest of the crew. The noise was so loud—especially because of the proximity of the microphone to the dogs—that everyone had to cover their ears.

Nick stepped closer to the microphone, stuck his thumb and forefinger between his lips, and whistled. The whistle echoed through the town square.

The howling stopped and all nine dogs sat on their haunches, their full attention on Nick.

This time, when the crowd applauded, they did so cautiously, so as not to rile up the dogs again.

"Thank you, Silverwood," Nick said into the mic. "Thank you, Mayor McGuire. And thank you to my dog ensemble."

The crowd bubbled with laughter.

"It's my pleasure to accept this honor," he continued. "I want everyone to enjoy the festivities, so I'm going to keep this short and sweet. Behold, the lighting of the tree."

Nick pressed the button on a box sitting on the podium, and what seemed like a million lights sprung to life on the festival's Christmas tree.

The crowd *ooh*ed and *aah*ed and applauded at the glorious tree shining in the town square.

Holly felt her breath leave her for a moment as she took in the sight of it. A warm feeling ran through her, rich and comforting. She hadn't expected her emotions to come rushing to the surface like this, and so she sucked in a breath and smiled as she wiped a tear from her eye.

Chapter Seventeen

S he wasn't sure how long she'd been staring at the tree when she felt a breath on her neck. She turned her head slightly to find Nick behind her. He'd leaned closer and whispered, "That feeling you must be experiencing right now? That look on your face? That's not someone who doesn't want to celebrate Christmas."

She turned to him, attempting to push down her emotions. "The tree looks great. And congratulations on being the one to light it. What an honor."

"Thank you," he said with a nod. "I was hoping you'd get swept up in the crowd's merriment."

"I definitely am."

He narrowed his eyes. "I know you've been struggling with inspiration, so …" He glanced around and then focused on her again. "I have an idea."

"What is it?" she asked.

"Lucy," he said, turning to Lucy while a playful grin appeared. "If you don't mind, I was wondering if I could steal Holly away for the rest of the evening."

"Sure! I don't mind. Sean's coming to meet me after work."
Lucy leaned closer to Holly. "You better call me tomorrow and fill
me in on the whatever this turns out to be."

Holly could barely answer her before Nick took her hand.

"I'd like to show you something," he said.

"Oh." She was very aware of her heartbeat as it quickened at
the touch of his hand. "All right."

With his hand secure around hers, he gestured with a jerk of
his head for her to follow.

Holly quickly looked back at Lucy, who smiled and winked at
her.

"Where are we going?" Holly asked once they were in a less
dense part of the crowd.

"Just someplace I go for inspiration. I figured it was worth a
shot to show it to you."

"Okay."

Cupid followed them through the crowd to Nick's SUV.

"Oh," Holly said. "This is your car?"

"Did you think I lumbered all around town in my big truck?"

"I guess I hadn't really thought about it. The truck is the only
thing I've seen you drive."

He nodded as he opened the passenger-side door for her. "Fair
enough."

She climbed into the car and heard the back open. A glance
over her shoulder showed her that Cupid was happy to be in the
back. She fought the urge to wring her hands as her senses
heightened.

Nick slid into the driver's seat and smiled at her. "I'm not kidnapping you, in case you're worried."

"Said the kidnapper to throw off his victims." She let out a nervous laugh.

"I promise you're in good hands." He started the engine and began driving.

Holly tried to distract herself from thinking about his hands by twisting her neck to check on Cupid.

"That was something up there on stage," she said, "with the whole family of dogs."

He chuckled as he maneuvered the car along a curvy road. "Yeah, it was unexpected, but not the first time it's happened."

"I'm surprised the stage didn't collapse with all the dogs up there."

"Not to worry, Holly. I built it to stand strong."

"You built the stage?" She waved her hand dismissively. "Never mind. Of course you did."

He kept his eyes on the road but widened his smile.

"By the way …" Nick cleared his throat. "My sister would like you to join us at her place for dinner tomorrow. If you don't have any plans, that is."

"That's so sweet. Yes, I accept."

He glanced at her with a smile. Holly wondered if it was relief that removed the shadow from his face.

She shifted her attention to the starlit sky. The sprinkling of twinkling lights hovering above snowy trees was hypnotic, and she wondered if this was what Nick wanted her to see. After a few more minutes, Nick pulled the car into a clearing and parked.

"We're here?" Holly asked.

"Yeah, come see." Nick got out of the car and opened the back.

As Cupid ran off in the dark, Nick closed the back of the car, appearing with a duffle bag slung over his shoulder.

"What's that?" she asked.

"Just a shovel and some rope." He bit his cheek but couldn't hold back the laughter. "I'm kidding."

She was about to shoot off another question when their real destination came into view.

Before them sat a breathtaking frozen lake, spreading out as far as she could see with a gorgeous view of the mountains at the far end, all under the canopy of bright stars and a blanket of clear, dark blue. Cupid sniffed around in the snow by the edge of the lake.

She gasped, a tingle fluttering over her skin. "Wow."

"This is one of my favorite places to be," Nick said.

"This is beautiful, Nick." Holly placed a hand on her heart.

"It's quite an experience to skate out there under the stars."

"Oh, wow. Yeah, I bet."

"Want to give it a try?"

She laughed. "Yeah, sure. I'm sure I can buy some skates in town and—"

"No, I mean now." He tilted his head.

She furrowed her brow. "What? How?"

He unzipped the duffle bag and pulled out two pairs of ice skates.

A breath of a laugh escaped her lips. "Um ..."

"The second pair is Rachel's. She made a bet with me that they'd fit you."

"Oh! Well, now it makes sense. She kept looking at my feet

when I came into the shop."

Nick gestured to a bench near the shore of the lake. "Let's put them on."

Cupid followed them and sniffed at every piece of grass and pile of dried leaves he found. When they reached the bench, Nick unlaced his boots. Holly followed suit and unzipped hers. He handed her Rachel's skates, which she slipped her feet into, surprised that they fit perfectly.

"Now, I don't know how inspiration works from a technical point of view," Nick said as he laced up his skates, "but I'm a big believer that feeling good can lead to being creative."

She pulled on the laces on her skates, making sure they were tight enough to keep her steady on the ice. "Maybe you're right. I might be letting disappointment discourage me."

"Sometimes we're disappointed about things because we're looking at them the wrong way."

She was having a difficult time getting the tension right. Nick kneeled down and helped her with the lacing.

"It's hard to look at failure the wrong way," she said.

"The only way you fail at something is if you don't get back up when you get knocked down." He looked up at her as he tied the knot in her skate.

"I know you're right," she said as she stood. "But I can't help but feel like a little girl who's dreams got too big."

He stood and took her hand. "At least you did it. Reached for your dreams. Most people I know are afraid to even try. Sometimes you have to reevaluate what your dreams really are. Maybe there's a reason things didn't turn out exactly as you had planned."

Holly looked down at their joined hands. "Maybe."

"Ready to give this a try?"

Their eyes locked, and a rush of warmth flooded her body. "I think I am."

He helped her to the edge of the lake and slid onto the ice with ease. He gracefully turned to her and held his hand out. Holly took a deep breath and exhaled slowly.

"It's fine," he said. "I'm right here."

"Yeah." She smiled at him sweetly. "Yeah, you are."

She took two rickety steps before she got more of a feel for the movement. Her hair flowed gently behind her in the cool air. She paused to reach into her pocket and retrieve her hat. At the lake's edge, Cupid rolled around in the snow, huffing as if some of it got in his nose.

"You've skated before, haven't you?" Nick asked.

"Yes, but only on man-made rinks. I don't think my parents ever took me here. Probably because my mother could get paranoid about everything. If I were to skate on a real lake, she would have completely freaked out with worry."

"There's nothing to worry about. The ice is thick. It's completely safe." To demonstrate how true his statement was, Nick turned and raced in a wide circle, gliding upon the ice as if he'd been born with blades for feet. Completing his circle, he skidded to a stop in front of her, kicking up bits of ice.

"All right." She skated toward him, feeling a bit unstable only because of how weak her knees were. It was all Nick's fault.

But his smile …

She got the hang of it in no time and was soon floating along the ice alongside him. The wind rushed by her face, and the snow sparkled on the mountaintops in the moonlight. She felt free. And with Nick nearby, she felt at peace. For a few minutes, the rest of the world disappeared. It was just the two of them, floating along on the ice.

When her blade caught a stray pebble, she stumbled, flailing her arms as she tried to retain her balance. Nick swooped in, reached out, and caught her arm, gently pulling her to him.

"I've got you," he said, his hand on the small of her back.

He didn't know how right he was. Her mind's eye snapped a picture of this moment.

She gazed into his eyes. "Maybe we should sit down for a bit? Catch our breaths?"

"You bet." He took her hand and led her back to the bench.

They sat close together, and Holly gazed out at the panorama of stars.

Though she didn't want to think about Grayson, he did come to mind. But only as a reflection of how wrong he'd been for her. She'd never felt as comfortable and at ease as she was with Nick. She could be herself around Nick, and she didn't feel the constant need to prove herself. No matter how much personality and social status he had, she didn't feel like she had to compete to keep up with him or outdo him. She wasn't intimidated by him; she was excited by him.

She turned to face him and found him deep in thought. Her smile slowly faded.

"Nick, I know about your father."

She heard his long breath. He tilted his head and found her

eyes.

"I didn't get it before," she continued, "but now I know that he's the reason you work so hard."

"He's most of the reason, yeah." His eyes went to Cupid, who was sniffing around in the snow. "But it's also because of my mom."

"Oh?"

"Yeah, she was always keeping busy, doing things to help other people. There was always a project she was working on, and she never seemed to tire. But I guess she was keeping busy to hide the cancer."

Holly placed a hand on his shoulder. "I'm so sorry."

"I guess I thought I was keeping her alive by taking over for her. Running the tree farm and The Gingerbread House. Joining committees I knew she'd join. I know I need to slow down sometimes. Rachel actually had to talk me out of running for mayor."

Holly let out a small laugh. "It's a good thing she did. You'd burn out if you took that on too."

"Yeah, probably." His eyes flitted over her face. "I wasn't trying to keep my dad's illness a secret from you. I'm the kind of guy who prefers action to words, keeping in motion rather than worrying about a problem. And I figured you would hear about his condition eventually."

She took his hand in both of hers. "If there's anything I can do …"

"Thanks." He squeezed her hand. "We're taking care of him. Our main concern is making sure he can continue his treatment.

If he gets his medication, he'll be all right."

"Yeah, he told me how much it's costing him."

"Well, he tends to overshare," Nick said, shaking his head. "But actually, that's one of the reasons we're determined to win this tree decorating contest."

A wrinkle formed between her eyes. "The statewide one?"

"That's the one. The cash prize would be enough to keep him covered for probably ten years. And the whole town voted and agreed to donate the winnings to him so he could get the treatment he needs."

Holly's eyes widened. She shot up from the bench. "Well, then we better win!"

The corner of his mouth inched upward. "We?"

"Yeah." She wobbled, still on the blades of her skates.

Nick reached out and took her hands, standing up and closing some of the distance between them. "We," he repeated. "I like the sound of that."

Chapter Eighteen

Holly took in the view of the outside of the house, double checking to make sure she'd had the address right. It was a beautiful, two-story, modern home with walls of windows and a broad, low-pitched gable roof. The structure was white with accents of black used for the window and door frames. The home was set in a cozy part of Silverwood, with plenty of private land and a sprinkling of trees for good measure.

Getting out of her car, Holly pulled her coat tighter around her red dress. She hoped she had picked the right mixture of dressy and casual, having ignored Kim's suggestion of wearing something that showed more skin. Her boots clicked along the cobblestone walkway, and Holly took some deep breaths to calm herself.

"It's not a big deal," she said to herself. "It's just dinner. With friends. And the handsome hero of the town."

Taking one final calming breath, she shook out her arms and then rang the doorbell. The bell chimed to the tune of *Angels We Have Heard on High*, which brought a smile to Holly's face. A few barks emanated from inside the house.

When the door opened, Rachel greeted her with a grin. "Holly,

145

hello!"

Holly held up a long gift bag containing a bottle of wine. "Thank you for inviting me, Rachel. This is for you."

"Aw, that wasn't necessary, but thank you. Come on in."

Dasher and Cupid danced around Holly, sniffing at her legs as she stepped inside.

Rachel took her coat. "Come into the kitchen. I want you to meet my husband."

"I'd love to." Holly rubbed her hands together, wishing they weren't so sweaty. "You have a lovely home."

Rachel had an open kitchen layout that looked out onto the dining area. At the kitchen island, busying themselves over a couple of frying pans, were Nick and another man who Holly deduced was Rachel's husband. Nick watched her, a smile playing on his lips. She greeted him with a nod, welcoming the warm feeling that filled her at the sight of him.

"Eddie," Rachel said, going up to the men and stealing a baby carrot from the counter, "this is Holly. Holly, my husband Eddie."

Holly clasped her hands behind her back. "Nice to meet you."

"So, you're Nick's Holly." Eddie winked.

Holly and Nick caught each other's gaze before Nick turned his attention back to roasting vegetables.

Rachel playfully smacked Eddie's shoulder. "Cut it out, trouble-maker."

"Holly!" came a voice from the next room. Avery came running in and embraced Holly around her waist.

"Hi, Avery." Holly held her at arm's length. "Ooh, nice dress."

"Thank you." Avery gave her a fun curtsy. "So is yours."

"I've got to hand it to you, Avery. You've got great fashion sense."

"Do I hear an angel speaking?" Mr. Mason asked, coming into the room with a chuckle.

"Nicholas." Holly approached him and gave him a hug. She wasn't sure what had come over her, but it seemed fitting to embrace him. "I didn't know you were going to be here. What a pleasant surprise."

He leaned in closer. "To tell you the truth, I'm not even sure Rachel knew I'd be here." He let out a laugh, a hand on his jiggling belly.

"Oh, Dad." Rachel came over and gently nudged him. "Why don't you take these lovely ladies to the family room while we finish up dinner and set the table."

"Are you sure I can't help?" Holly asked.

"Go on." Rachel waved a hand. "We've got it covered."

"Yeah." Avery pulled on Holly's hand. "Come see our tree."

Cupid and Dasher barked at Avery's efforts to pull Holly into the other room. Holly quickly glanced at Nick, who smirked and waved at her with a spatula.

"Uncle Nick let me pick it out from the tree farm," Avery continued. "He even let me saw it a little."

"No way." Holly smiled at her. "I'm so jealous."

"She is a beauty," Mr. Mason said, stuffing his hands in his pockets and admiring the tree.

Holly had to agree. It was a perfect cut and was classily decorated. Holly spotted Avery's decoration she made in art school, and her heart warmed. "I love it."

"Nicky got you a nice one too." Mr. Mason tilted his head. "You manage to get it decorated yet?"

"Mostly." Holly grimaced. "I think I'm overthinking ornament placement. My mom is so much better at it than I am."

Holly's gaze was drawn to the fireplace, which crackled with a blazing fire. On the mantel sat a framed picture of a young Mr. Mason with his arm around a beautiful woman who resembled Rachel. Holly walked toward it and ran a finger down the side of the frame.

"That's Eleanor." Mr. Mason appeared next to her, his voice low and gentle.

"She's beautiful," Holly said.

"Oh, she was incredible." He gazed lovingly at his late wife's image. "She was a very passionate person. Loved volunteering, was obsessed with baking. Also liked to dabble in sewing and painting. She actually made that."

He gestured to a framed painting hanging above the sofa. It was a lovely landscape oil painting of a tropical island at sunset.

"Wow, that's some pretty good dabbling," Holly said.

"I think Avery's got her genes, as much as she loves art."

"That's awesome."

Holly wrapped her arms around herself as she took in the colors of the painting. She remembered how Nick spoke about his mother and all the things she did, the life she lived. He could tell she had been someone extremely special, and she'd been blessed to have such a loving family value her so much. It was no wonder where Nick got his drive from.

Rachel appeared in the doorway, wiping her hands on a dish

towel. "Dinner's ready. Let's eat."

Nick stood at the table, his hand on the back of a chair. "Here's your seat, Holly."

"Thank you." She paused before she sat down. "Baking, cooking, chivalry. It's like your vetting for some kind of superman prize."

"There's a quote from a Roman philosopher I like to think of as my motto. It goes: Waste no more time arguing about what a good man should be. Be one."

Holly gave him a nod. "I like that. Very wise and very fitting."

He pulled out her chair. "You look really nice, by the way."

She blushed. "Thanks. So do you."

She sat and ran her fingers along the red-oak tabletop, remembering he had made the piece of furniture for his sister. It was masterfully crafted and gorgeous.

Holly couldn't have been more satisfied with how the evening transpired. The food was delicious, and the dinner conversation was easy and uplifting. The occasional intense glances between Nick and herself made her want the evening to go on forever.

As Rachel and Eddie cleared the table—which they insisted they needed no help with—Avery showed Holly some tricks she'd taught Dasher. Nick sat beside Holly on the sofa, his leg touching hers.

"Avery," Rachel said, leaning against the doorway. "Time for bed."

Holly checked her phone to see what time it was and realized she'd been there for hours.

"Not until Uncle Nick plays us a song on his guitar," Avery whined.

"You play guitar?" Holly asked.

He smirked. "Maybe a little?"

"He's being modest again," Eddie said. "He's incredibly talented."

Holly gaped at Nick. "I'll say."

"Not tonight," Rachel said to Avery. "It's been a long evening and you've got to get your sleep."

Avery frowned. "Fine."

"Next time, kiddo," Nick told her.

Holly stood, taking that as her cue to leave as well. "I need to be heading home anyway."

Avery rushed over to her and hugged her. "It was great having you over, Holly. Come over any time you want."

Holly laughed. "That's awfully nice of you. Thanks."

"Goodnight, everyone!" Avery called.

As Avery ran off and up the stairs, Rachel approached Holly. "I've got to go up and make sure she brushes her teeth. But it was really nice having you over." She surprised Holly by giving her a hug. "And I agree with Avery. Come over any time."

Holly's heart felt so full she almost couldn't form words. "Thanks again for having me. It was perfect."

Eddie came over and hugged her as well. "I can see why Nick is taken with you. Don't be a stranger."

Nick was suddenly beside her. "I'll walk you to your car."

"Thanks."

She had been so warm and comfortable in Rachel's and Eddie's home that the blast of cold air hitting her when Nick opened the door surprised her. She buttoned her coat as the two of them walked toward her car.

When they reached it, she turned to him. "This was great. I'm glad we did this."

"Me too." His gaze flitted around her face.

"Oh, I have a present for Avery." She opened her car and pulled out the wrapped gift. "Will you put it under the tree for me?"

"Sure." His dimple appeared when he smiled. "That was nice of you."

"She's a great kid. With great taste." Holly gave him a half-shrug. "She's grown on me."

"I totally understand the feeling." The way he was looking into her eyes made Holly wonder if he was really talking about her. "What about Silverwood?"

"What do you mean?"

"Has Silverwood grown on you as well?"

She raised her brows, not sure how to answer.

He shrugged. "Just wondering, since you mentioned you might sell your place. It would be awfully nice if you stuck around a while." His gaze intensified. "A long while."

"Well, as it stands, I've put off trying to find a real estate agent." She glanced up at the night sky. "I have to admit, Silverwood does have a way of touching one's heart."

"So that means …?"

They were standing so close to each other she could feel the warmth radiating off of him.

"I don't know. We'll see." Letting out a trembling breath, she forced herself to turn toward her car. "Goodnight, Nick." She looked up at him once she was in her seat, finding it hard to break her stare.

His eyes seemed to twinkle. "Goodnight, Holly. Drive safe."

Chapter Nineteen

The driveway at Emily's house was already fully occupied. Holly parked on the side of the road and checked her reflection in the visor mirror. When her phone began to buzz, she figured it was Emily asking where she was. Instead, Kim's name appeared on her phone screen.

For a second, panic found a way into Holly's brain. Had Grayson somehow manipulated Kim into telling him where she was, and Kim was now calling to warn her that he was coming to find her? Making a fist with one hand, she pressed the button to accept the call.

"Kim?"

"Holly! Hi!" She didn't sound upset.

Holly released her fist and placed her hand on her heart to slow it down. "Is everything okay?"

"Better than okay, Holly. I found you a new agent. Am I the bestest friend ever or what?"

"What?" Holly's brow furrowed. "Kim, slow down. What are you talking about?"

"I'm talking about your ticket back to New York. I mean, I

know you've already given up your apartment and all, but you can totally stay with me until you settle back in."

"Kim! Back up. I'm lost."

"An agent, Holly. I found you an agent. And once we get you signed you can move back to the city and reclaim your throne in the art world."

"Wait. Who's the agent?"

"You know Derrick?"

Holly laughed. "Your hairstylist is an agent?"

"No, no. Derrick knows a guy—he does his hair too—and that guy is the agent."

"For artists?"

"Duh, of course. I made sure. And he's willing to meet with you to talk about representation."

"Wait." Holly felt flustered. She placed her free hand on her cheek and shook her head. "What's this guy's name and who does he represent?"

"Cooper something? I wrote it down, but I can't find the paper right now. Anyway, he remembers your name and would love to have a meeting."

"Does he have other clients?" A tiny ache was forming in her temple. "I don't think I've heard of anyone named Cooper."

"Well, he *is* new. His client list is small, but doesn't that mean he has more time to concentrate on you? Come on, Holly, this could be your next big break. Should I tell him you're interested?"

Holly bit her lip. Someone walked by her car and glanced at her as she made her way to Emily's door. This wasn't the time to make rash decisions "I don't know."

"You can at least meet with him." There was Kim's whiny voice again. "But it has to be in person, and you should bring your best pieces of art."

"Yeah. Um, let me think about it, ok?"

"Yay! I can look up ticket prices for you to fly out after New Year's. I'll text you with more information."

"All right. Text me his name, too, so I can look him up." Holly tucked a strand of hair away from her face. "Thanks, Kim."

"Anything for you, Holly-bear!"

As the call ended, Holly's mind swirled. She wasn't sure whether this agent Kim stumbled upon was legit or not. The art world wasn't something Kim was brushed up on, so she had her doubts. There were lots of people out there who swindled people without a second thought. But if Kim was right, and this was Holly's second chance …

Her thoughts suddenly went to Nick. And Avery and Rachel and Mr. Mason. Holly stared at Emily's door, feeling conflicted. She'd just gotten Lucy back as well. Was chasing a maybe worth the risk of losing everything she gained in Silverwood?

With a grunt, she pushed the thoughts of New York away and got out of her car. She didn't have to decide right then and there. She had to put Kim's surprise call on the back burner for now. Walking up the front walk, she cleared the worry from her face and told herself to focus on Lucy's baby shower.

Emily opened the door of her house and greeted Holly with a hug. She ushered her inside. "I'm so sorry about the short notice. I've been so busy with dealing with the school that it slipped my mind to invite you to Lucy's baby shower."

"No, it's fine." Holly waved a hand in dismissal. "I'm just glad I didn't miss it. Where can I put my gift?"

"We have a table set up right over there." Emily gestured to some women who were conversing in the kitchen and making finger sandwiches. "That's Abigail, Cindy, and Elisa—close friends of Lucy. Elisa is actually her sister-in-law."

The thin blonde smiled and gave Holly a friendly wave.

"Thanks for including me," Holly called out to them.

"Of course." Elisa gave her a nod before returning to her task.

"It's just a small gathering," Emily explained. "With Christmas and all, a few of Lucy's friends were out of town or simply couldn't fit it into their schedules. But she'll be touched that you're here."

"You know what I just realized? This is the first time I've been to your house. As a kid, I never thought I'd get a chance to see my teacher's home. It's nice."

"Well, thank you."

Holly looked around the room, her gaze landing on a tower of cupcakes displayed on the sideboard. She immediately thought of Nick.

"Are those from The Gingerbread House?" she asked, pointing to the delectable-looking, pink-frosted treats.

"Of course." Emily winked. "Lucy's favorite. I wouldn't get them from anywhere else, and I'm simply not as able with baking as I am with a paint brush."

"Well, everything looks great." Holly admired the baby banner and the themed napkins. "She's going to love it."

For some reason, she gravitated toward the cupcake display. She didn't even know if it was Nick who had made them, but the mere fact that something existed in the room that had a connection to him made something flutter in Holly's belly. She had the strong desire to eat one, just to feel somehow close to him.

Holly turned her attention back to Emily. "When is Lucy getting here?"

Emily glanced at the grandfather clock near the dining room table. "In about half an hour, give or take. Which reminds me: would you mind helping me finish the diaper cake?"

Holly blinked. "The what?"

Emily let out a laugh. "It's a tower of diapers and bibs assembled in the shape of a three-tier cake, usually topped with something like a stuffed animal or a rattle or some toy for the baby. I've already started it, but need some help finishing it."

"Of course. Let's do it."

As they began rolling up the tiny diapers, Holly contemplated telling Emily what she'd heard in the school parking lot the other day.

"So," Emily said, interrupting Holly's train of thought. She kept her voice low so the others wouldn't hear. "Lucy tells me you and Nick Mason have been getting along."

Holly's skin grew hot. She glanced over her shoulder to check on the other women, but they had disappeared deep into the kitchen.

"We've … hung out a few times."

"Hung out?" Emily narrowed her eyes. "You think you can fool me, but I'm old and wise. The mere mention of his name and you start to glow."

Holly let go of the diaper she'd been rolling and covered her cheeks with her hands. "Oh no. Is it that obvious?"

Emily tilted her head. "What are you afraid of?"

Holly shook her head, dropping her hands at her sides. "I don't know. Failure, I guess. I just got out of a failed relationship. I feel like I failed at my career. I don't know if I could handle being let down again."

"There's a flaw in your thinking, though." Emily placed a hand on her shoulder. "First, I think you're putting too much pressure on yourself regarding your career. I think you're concentrating on the money instead of the feeling. The connection to your art, that's what counts. Secondly, regarding relationships and being let down again, you're so afraid of falling that you're not allowing yourself to be lifted up."

It took a moment for Holly to absorb her words. To really understand the meaning.

"Tell me about it." Emily elbowed her. "The *hanging out.*"

"Well, he took me ice skating under a starlit sky."

"Ah, yes. I know the frozen lake from my younger years. Very romantic."

"It was. Yeah." Holly rolled the next diaper and handed it to Emily. "And he brought me a Christmas tree. Out of the blue. And last night, I had dinner with his family."

"Sounds like more than just hanging out to me."

Holly shrugged, a small smile playing on her lips. "Maybe. But what would I be getting myself into? I don't even know if I'm staying in Silverwood." The call from Kim came back to her train of thought. She hadn't had anything pulling her away from Silverwood before, but now she was having her doubts about staying.

"Sometimes we need to trust we're being led down the right path before we understand the destination."

But which path is the right one?

Holly gave Emily a sideways smile. "You know what? You really are wise."

"You forgot 'old'."

They laughed, and Emily tied a pink ribbon around the top tier of the cake.

"So how did that interview go?" Holly asked.

Emily frowned. "It was a bust. She wasn't right for the job. She kept going on and on about stencils."

"Seriously?"

"Yeah, she even pulled out some catalog and showed me her favorites."

Holly laughed. "I mean, I don't want to judge what other people call art, but … stencils?"

She and Emily burst into a short fit of laughter.

"Well, I guess the search continues, then?" Holly asked.

Emily tilted her head. "I suppose so."

"She's here!" Elisa said, rushing out from the kitchen.

Emily nodded and patted Holly on her shoulder. "Thank you for helping me, Holly. And I hope you are able to come to a decision. But for now, let's celebrate Lucy's baby."

Chapter Twenty

Holly stepped back, smiling at her Christmas tree. She finally finished decorating it, having abandoned the theory that it had to be perfect. It was liberating to stop overthinking and just wing it. And her tree looked great. Authentic. Perhaps she needed to do the same with her art.

Turning on her heel, she grabbed her camera and her coat. She decided to go out and shoot as many pictures as she could, no matter how random and obscure they were.

As she headed out to her car, she caught sight of Mr. and Mrs. Miranelli hunched over in the snow in their yard. Mrs. Miranelli spotted her, stood up straight, and waved.

Holly felt obligated to approach her. If nothing else, she was curious as to what they were concentrating so hard on in their yard. "Hello, Mrs. Miranelli. Mr. Miranelli."

"Is that really Holly St. Ives?" Mr. Miranelli stood from his crouched position.

Holly saw that he'd been repairing their fence. Mrs. Miranelli was obviously supervising.

"Yep. It's me," Holly replied. "How are you, Mr. Miranelli?"

He scratched at his wool hat with his hammer. "Oh, you know how it is. The missus is keeping me on my toes."

"Oh, Henry." Mrs. Miranelli chuckled. "This is the first you've been on your feet all month, let alone your toes."

"Yeah, yeah, woman." Mr. Miranelli snuck Holly a wink and then turned back to his task. "You want this fence fixed or what?"

Mrs. Miranelli shook her head. "Where are you headed today?"

"I'm looking for inspiration." Holly lifted her camera.

"Sounds like fun. Hope you find some. But, dear, please be careful. There's talk of a storm coming in. Not sure when it will hit."

"Thanks, I will."

Holly ran back to her car and ventured off to find her muse. She took a turn away from town, heading uphill. She wondered how high up the mountain she could go. She felt as if she were chasing the sun.

She'd been driving for almost an hour before she found a place to stop. It was a gravelly spot beside the road right before a big curve going up the mountain. There were fields of snow and a scattering of trees. Aside from being a beautiful spot in nature, there wasn't anything in particular that was special about the place.

"Okay. No being picky," she said to herself. "Everything is a possibility."

She hiked through the snow and took pictures of everything she could, without restricting herself.

"Follow the path. Follow the path." She ended up on an unmarked trail between widely spaced-out trees.

The sun was at an angle that created shadows of the trees on the snowbanks, giving the land an almost blue-ish tint. Holly snapped the landscape, zooming in on a cluster of evergreens far off up the mountain.

Movement through her lens made her jump. She wasn't alone up here.

She used the camera to figure out who was out there, forcing herself to keep her breaths steady. When she saw a couple of squirrels race across the land and a Malamute charging after them, she had to laugh out loud.

Cupid? Was Nick here?

She heard a whistle, and Cupid bounded through the snow, kicking up flakes left and right. Holly followed his movement with her camera, snapping pictures, and traced him back to Nick. Nick pet Cupid on the head and then threw a long stick far off for Cupid to chase.

Holly's focus stayed on Nick, and her finger tapped down on the camera's button. She hadn't meant to, but she'd caught Nick mid-throw.

"Well, the damage is already done," she whispered to herself and proceeded to snap a few more pictures.

Nick turned his head.

Holly lowered the camera and waved to him. She couldn't see his expression, but from his stance, Holly was guessing he was surprised to see her.

Trudging through the snow, they made their way toward each other. Cupid barked and headed her way as well. Holly's breaths were heavy, and her heart was pounding by the time she was close enough to see Nick's face clearly. Cupid reached her first, nearly knocking her down when he jumped up to greet her.

"Holly, I … This is some kind of crazy coincidence."

Her hair flew around her head. She tucked her stray strands under her winter hat. "Yeah. I didn't know you'd be up here. I didn't even know where *here* was until now."

"I like to come here with Cupid sometimes. Him being a snow dog, I figure he needs to do what he was born to do and run wild once in a while. Burn up his energy. Terrify a few squirrels."

"He looks like he loves it."

"He does."

A Northern Shrike landed a few yards away and chirped. Cupid barked and ran after it. It took off, its wings kicking up snow.

"I see you're hunting down inspiration again." Nick tugged on her camera strap.

"Always. I, uh, got a couple shots of you playing with Cupid. I hope that's okay."

"You shot me?"

She smiled. "Guilty."

"Let me see."

For a second, she couldn't move. *Come on, Holly. Pull yourself together.*

His hand was open in front of her.

"Okay." She took the strap off her neck and handed him the camera.

Holly watched his face as he scrolled through the pictures. When his dimple appeared, her heart swelled.

His eyes found hers. "Let's get one of us together."

"Of us? Oh. Um, okay."

She instinctively removed her hat and tucked it into her coat pocket. She was only able to run her fingers over her hair once before Nick put his arm around her waist and pulled her next to him. Her breath left her for a moment as he pressed up against her and aimed the camera at their heads.

Holly laughed. "How do you know if we're in the shot?"

"I don't. Taking a risk is half the fun."

Click.

"A couple more, just to be safe. His hand tightened on her hip.

Taking a deep breath, she could smell his soap. Or was it his shampoo? Whatever it was, it was nice.

He handed the camera back to her. "Let's see how we did."

She laughed when the pictures were off-center, either part of her head or part of his cut off.

"I can't believe it," she said. "There's actually something you're not perfect at."

What started as a gasp of shock ended in loud laughter. Holly couldn't help but join in.

As they sobered from their bout of hysterics, Nick studied Holly's face. She was transfixed by his stare. Her mind swirled when it seemed as if they were leaning closer and closer together.

The ding of her phone announcing she'd just received a message interrupted their gaze.

Holly cleared her throat as she pulled her phone out of her pocket and checked her screen. Her jaw tightened and she shoved her phone back in her pocket, her mood ruined. She hadn't even read the message, but she'd seen enough.

"Everything all right?" Nick asked, narrowing his eyes.

"Yeah," she lied. She tried to smile, but it just wasn't working.

"Holly, you know you can tell me anything."

She sighed. "Um, okay. I really didn't want to bring it up, but, uh, I have an ex-boyfriend who keeps finding ways to call or message me. I've blocked him, but he just keeps using other friends' phones to … well, to harass me."

Nick frowned. "Sounds like a stalker."

Holly covered her face with her hands. "Right? See, I've got baggage. It's horrible."

Nick snickered, gently tugging her hands away from her face. "We've all got baggage, Holly."

Her shoulders dropped. "I'm hoping if I ignore him long enough, he'll eventually leave me alone. I just want him to stop ruining things for me."

"Don't let him. Focus on something else. If he's got any sense, he'll get bored and leave you alone for good."

"The not having sense part worries me."

"I can send my killer dog over to convince him," he joked.

"Well, his face does resemble that of a squirrel's."

Nick placed a hand on her shoulder. "Well, if there's any way I can serve as a distraction, just let me know."

A smile slowly crept up on her face. Her hand came up and rested on his chest. "You're doing a pretty good job so far."

Snowflakes landed on their faces. Holly looked up at the sky, which had darkened with clouds.

"Mrs. Miranelli mentioned a storm was coming in." Holly hung the camera strap back around her neck. "I think we probably better get off the mountain before it hits."

"I think you're right. Where are you parked?"

She pointed. "Down there a bit. You?"

"Oh, up over that hill." He gestured in the opposite direction. "But what kind of gentleman would I be if I didn't offer to walk you to your car?"

"You really don't have to."

He smirked. "I know."

As they walked toward her car, Cupid barked and ran past them, as if he knew exactly where they were going.

"Are you coming to the festival tomorrow evening? We're holding a baked goods auction to raise some money."

She smiled up at him. "I'll definitely be there."

When they reached her car, her phone dinged again. Without thinking, she whipped it out of her coat pocket and checked the screen.

He leaned forward a little. "Is that him?"

"What?" Holly had momentarily forgotten about Grayson. "Oh! No, it's my friend Kim. She's sending me airline ticket prices."

Nick's brows pulled together. "For …?"

"Um … New York."

His face sobered and he took a step back. "Oh."

Holly's smile disappeared, and she tucked her phone away. "You see, she, uh, wanted to set up a meeting for me with this agent she knows. Or knows through someone else. It's a little complicated. Anyway, I'm not even sure—"

He waved a hand in dismissal. "No. Of course. You do what you need to do. I just, uh—" He trailed off, stuffing his hands in his coat pockets as he took a couple steps back, his eyes went elsewhere, as if he were deep in thought.

"Nick."

He shook his head. "See, now you've made it awkward for me, because I don't want to sound like your ex. I'm not the kind of guy to hold you back or be controlling. If your career is important to you, I get that. It's just …"

Cupid let out a small whine, as if he could feel Nick's emotions.

Holly's chest began to ache. She could see Nick was hurt. But he wouldn't look her in the eye.

"It's probably a long shot anyway," she said. "I mean, I didn't give her a definite answer that I would go."

"Which means you didn't tell her no." He let out a sigh. "I don't know, I guess I'm just a little shocked."

"I told you I wasn't sure how long I'd be in Silverwood."

"I know. But we were just getting close. There was this vibe between us. And Avery and my dad and my sister. I guess I was foolish to think you'd be happy here. That we … That I would be enough."

She opened her mouth to respond, but she wasn't sure what she wanted to say. Because she wasn't sure what she wanted to do. She didn't want to lose Nick and his family. And Lucy and Emily. But she also hadn't figured out what she wanted to do about her dream.

The snow began to fall faster and harder. The wind picked up, whipping her hair around her.

"You better go," Nick said, his face stoic. "It's going to start coming down hard. Get home safe."

"Okay, well." She wasn't sure what to say or do. She only knew she didn't want to leave his side. But the icy wind had other ideas. "Drive safe?"

He nodded, his eyes meeting hers for a split second before he turned away.

Holly watched him for a moment, a shiver shaking her to the core. She waited a moment, wishing he would turn around, but he continued up the hill. As more wet snowflakes hit her in the face, she turned and climbed into her car, the gloomy sky a reflection of dark cloud that suddenly filled her heart.

Chapter Twenty-One

Holly aimed her phone at her tree.

"Oh, yes," her mother said through the speakerphone. "Wow, that's very nice. Good job, honey."

Holly clicked the symbol to change the camera's focus back to her. "Thanks, Mom."

"So, who gave you the tree again?"

"Nick Mason?" Holly shifted on the couch, tucking her feet underneath herself. "His mom owned The Gingerbread House … before she passed away."

"Oh. I love that place. Delicious cupcakes."

Holly giggled. "Yeah, they're still delicious. Nick owns it now." She bit the inside of her cheek, the memory of their fight on the mountain sending waves of acid to her gut.

"Hmm. This *Nick* sounds like a good guy."

Holly's toes curled. "He is, Mom."

"Then why are you frowning?"

Holly shook her head and forced a smile. "No reason. I just miss you."

"Aw, miss you too, honey."

There was some background noise, and her mother turned her focus away from the camera. Holly waited until she spoke again.

"Okay, honey. Your Auntie Lita says we're leaving for Uncle Jun's house now."

"All right. Tell everyone Merry Christmas for me."

Her mom blew kisses to the phone and waved. "Merry Christmas, Holly. I love you."

"Love you too!"

The screen changed back to her mom's contact page, showing that the call had ended. Holly checked the time and stood. Not only was Nick expecting her at the baked-good auction, but so were Lucy and Emily.

Besides, she had to see if Nick was still upset with her. She felt the need to sit down with him and talk about New York. She still wasn't sure what she wanted to do, but she knew that that's what Nick was upset about. In his eyes, Holly should have known what she wanted. Because if the answer wasn't Silverwood—if the answer wasn't Nick—then he probably wouldn't want to invest any more of his precious time in her.

The wind was harsh when she stepped outside. Tiny bits of ice pierced her face the entire walk from the front door to the car. Even sitting in the car with the door shut, the wind's howl was unbearably loud. Holly had to grip the steering wheel tightly to navigate the strong winds and icy snow.

By the time she arrived at the festival, sweat had formed at her temples. She was glad to have finally parked and gotten out of the car. Though the winds were still turbulent in the town square, there wasn't any ice rain pelting her in the face.

She pulled her hat down more snug over her head and winced against the unforgiving wind. Keeping her eye on the marshmallow roof of the Gingerbread House, she trudged forward toward her goal. If she could just reach it before the wind blew her away, she knew she'd be fine.

When she reached her destination, she let out a sigh of relief. A thrill ran through her when she spotted Nick. He was arranging boxes on the small back counter in the stand. The boxes were the same design as the welcome box she'd received from Nick. Would he even acknowledge her if she said hello? She doubted Nick could turn cold-hearted toward her over this. Could he?

A familiar face suddenly appeared at the service counter. "Hi! What can I get you?"

Nick turned, his eyes lighting up when he spotted Holly.

"Thanks, Viola." Nick placed a hand on her shoulder. "She's with me."

Holly smiled. She liked the sound of that. "Hey, you look busy."

"Most of the hard work is already done." He leaned forward on the counter, his eyes flitting over her face. "Give me a second. I'll come out and join you."

"Sure." Her voice quivered. It matched the frantic beating of her heart.

She looked around while she waited, shivering against the cold as snowflakes sped sideways in the air. She hoped the storm would hold off until the auction was over.

When Nick came out, he handed her a cup of hot chocolate. "Thought you could use this."

"Thanks." She held the cup closer to her chin. The steam rose and warmed her face. "So …" She cleared her throat. "You're not still mad at me?"

Nick took a deep breath and let it out slowly. "I was upset, yes. But now I've got another task on my to-do list."

"Oh, yeah? What's that?"

"Convincing you to stay."

"Nick—"

"Let's get closer to the stage." He took her by the hand. "I think the auction's going to start soon."

This time is wasn't the hot chocolate warming her, but Nick's touch. She forced herself to take steady breaths as they wound through the crowd hand in hand.

"Did you manage to get the sleigh set up?" she asked.

"Not quite yet. The red carpet was delivered this morning, but I've had to wait until the auction is over and the space is cleared so we can lay it out. I've got the sleigh on my truck, ready to be unloaded once the carpet is in position. Though, if this storm picks up, no one will be able to tell there's a carpet there at all. Guess we didn't have to buy the fake snow."

Holly blinked away snowflakes that landed on her lashes. "Probably not."

"Rachel's going to affix some twinkling lights to it and make it look great. And my dad and Avery have been wrapping empty boxes to fill the back of the sleigh. We'll put them in tomorrow after the storm clears.

"Sounds amazing." Holly sipped her hot drink, imagining what the set up would look like.

"Oh, and the best part—" Nick stopped and turned to her. "My dad's going to sit on the driver's bench, complete with a Santa suit. And Rachel found a dog sled harness for nine dogs, believe it or not. We're going to get Cupid and the others hooked up right before the judges come tomorrow. Maybe it will pull some weight with the judges. Excuse the pun."

Holly laughed. "Good one. I see what you did there. But, yeah, I can totally see that scoring some extra points. I mean, I can't wait to see it myself."

"Hey, you two," came a familiar voice.

Holly turned to find Lucy approaching with a tall man wearing glasses and a ski hat.

"Lucy, hi." Holly wiped snow from her face.

"Holly, this is my husband Sean."

Sean reached out to shake her hand. She reluctantly let go of Nick's hand, since her other hand was holding the hot chocolate.

"Hi, Sean." After she shook his hand, she wasn't sure if she should return her hand to Nick's. As soon as she dropped her hand at her side, Nick intertwined his fingers with hers, solving that puzzle.

"So good to meet you," Sean said. "Lucy goes on and on about you. Says you're the most famous person she knows."

"Oh." Holly wrinkled her brow and laughed. "Well, nice to meet you too. And, Lucy—way to put the pressure on."

"I can't wait to bid on your cupcakes, Nick." Lucy eyed her husband. "Sean promised I could have the whole box to myself."

"Wait." Sean raised a brow. "When did I agree to that?"

While Lucy and Sean playfully argued, Nick leaned in close to

Holly and whispered, "By the way, don't bid on anything. I'll gladly make you anything you want."

"But I want to help," she whispered back.

"Believe me, you've already helped. More than you know."

Feedback screeched through the speakers as Mrs. Miranelli switched on the mic on the podium.

"Sorry about that." Mrs. Miranelli adjusted her wooly hat and smiled at the crowd.

"I didn't know she was hosting the event," Holly said.

"This was all her idea," Nick told her. "I'm pretty sure she's rigged it so she gets the best item up for bids."

"Welcome, everyone, to the Silverwood Christmas Festival Baked Goods Auction. We're going to see how long we can, uh, weather the storm." Mrs. Miranelli chuckled at her own joke. "We'll hold out as long as we can manage under the circumstances. Our wonderful bakers have put in a lot of hard work for this event, so we're going to do what we can to get their masterpieces into your hungry hands."

The crowd applauded, and Nick glanced at Holly with a smile.

"We've got some mouth-watering goodies up for bid, and all proceeds, as you know, are going to a worthy cause. We're going to start off the auction with an extra-large tin of my very own Christmas cookies."

Holly's eyes widened. She glanced at Nick and bit her cheek to keep from laughing. He rubbed at his beard to hide the small laugh he let out.

The crowd seemed eager to donate, and the bidding went quickly. Though it interested Holly to see how enthusiastic the town was to pitch in to a good cause, she couldn't take her mind off how right it felt to have Nick holding her hand.

A downright bidding war erupted when The Gingerbread House's cupcake boxes went up for bids. The crowd got louder, and the bids grew larger. It was as if the heavy snowfall and severe winds didn't faze them. The excitement was contagious, and Holly squeezed Nick's hand in anticipation of how much they were raising because of him.

"And now," Mrs. Miranelli announced, "we've come to the last item on the auction schedule. Our crème de la crème of the event, the Deluxe Megabox of—"

The wind was so strong it knocked the microphone from the podium. The Christmas tree swayed, its branches pitching as ornaments fell and broke on the ground. The crowd let out gasps and shrieks. Holly had to hold down her hat, and Mrs. Miranelli's scarf was swept up by the storm, flying off above the crowd.

"Let's not panic," Mrs. Miranelli called out, frantically trying to retrieve the mic. "If everyone would kindly evacuate the square in a calm manner—"

A loud crack sounded, and the crowd began to scream. Holly felt the crowd push in on her. Nick took hold of her and moved her back out of the way. The Christmas tree toppled. Barks echoed in the air as the tree fell to the side and crashed into the roof of the churro stand. Its lights blinked out. In the next second, flames covered the top of the tree. It had hit the fryer when it broke through the stand's roof and caught fire.

"Call the fire department!" Nick took off, yelling directions as he rushed toward the stand. In a flash, he'd found a fire extinguisher and began dousing the flames.

"Holly, are you all right?" Mr. Mason appeared beside her, holding tight to Avery.

"Yes." She had to raise her voice over all the noise. Over the pounding of her own heart. "Let's get Avery somewhere safe."

They moved back away from the chaos as Nick successfully put out the fire. Black smoke rose from the damaged tree, clouding over the falling snow.

Rachel called her father over to where she was standing, under the awning of The Gingerbread House. Avery rushed into her arms and hugged her, her eyes wide and her lips set into a frown. Beside Rachel, Cupid and Dasher whined, panting and watching the turbulent incident unfold.

Mr. Mason wiped at his brow with his coat sleeve. "Oh, my Lord."

Holly searched for Nick finding him escorting the churro stand workers to safety. Luckily, it seemed no one was injured.

Nick's mouth was set in a straight line as he glanced back at the fallen tree. Acid filled Holly's stomach. It was ruined. Their chance at getting Mr. Mason's treatment had gone up in flames.

Chapter Twenty-Two

"Goodness!" Emily rushed up to them, holding on to her scarf. "What did I miss?"

"The Christmas tree fell down," Avery told her.

Holly wiped away the snowflakes that were stuck to her lashes. "It caught fire. Nick put it out, but the tree is ruined."

"Oh no." Emily winced against the wind and put a comforting hand on Mr. Mason's shoulder.

"Here comes Uncle Nick." Avery let go of her mom and placed her hands together under her chin. Dasher and Cupid ran up to Nick, whining and wagging their tails. Holly could see in Avery's eyes that she was hoping for good news.

"What's the verdict?" Mr. Mason asked when Nick reached them, but his tone told Holly that he already knew the answer.

Nick couldn't look him in the eye. He scratched the back of his neck, frowning. "It's ruined. I'm so sorry."

Mr. Mason slowly nodded. He patted his son on his back and offered a small smile. "There's always next year, Nicky."

Holly felt as if her heart had been hollowed out by something sharp and unforgiving. She couldn't wrap her mind around the fact that they had to throw the towel in.

She couldn't.

She wouldn't.

"No," she said, her hands tightened into fists. "No, there's got to be something we can do."

Nick placed a hand on the small of her back. "There's not. There's no time."

"The contest board is coming tomorrow," Rachel added.

Holly wrung her hands. "Aren't there any trees at the tree lot?"

Nick shook his head. "We've sold out."

"It's the day before Christmas Eve." Mr. Mason sighed. "The lot's been completely cleared."

Holly turned to Nick and grabbed his arms. "What about the tree farm?"

Nick blinked. "What about it?"

"We should go get a tree." Holly stared at him with wide eyes.

"Cut and net a tree? Now?"

"Yeah." What have we got to lose? We could band together and set it up."

"And have everything ready for the contest?" Nick scoffed. "That'll take all night."

"Not if we all pitch in." Holly glanced around. Everyone was gaping at her. "When are the judges coming?"

"Tomorrow at sunset," Rachel said.

"Then there's time. Come on, you guys are always telling me I've got to believe in the Christmas spirit. If there's ever a time to believe in miracles, it's now. We can do it."

Nick watched her, letting out a sigh. "There's no curbing your enthusiasm, is there?"

"If I learned anything about Silverwood, it's how united everyone in town is. I know everyone will pitch in. We can get it done in time. But first, we've got to get a tree."

The corners of Nick's mouth inched upward. "Okay. Let's do it."

Avery cheered. Cupid and Dasher barked.

"I'll tell Eddie to grab Sean," Rachel said. "They can help you at the tree farm."

Holly grabbed Nick's elbow. "I'm coming with you."

He gave her a nod. "Okay. Let's get to my truck."

"We'll take care of things here," Mr. Mason said. "Make sure the space is cleared and ready for you."

In a whirlwind of organizing, Nick, Holly, Sean, and Eddie banded together and headed for their vehicles. The snowfall was still heavy as they began their journey. Sean and Eddie followed Nick, Holly, and Cupid in Nick's truck, which still had the sleigh sitting in its bed.

The winds pushed against the truck as they maneuvered out of the town and toward Nick's tree farm. Holly fidgeted in her seat, as if movement would make things go faster. She told herself that this would work, as her heart beat strong and hard in her chest and something tightened in her stomach.

Holly's phone buzzed. She was surprised she could hear it through the howling wind. She looked at the screen. "Lucy says the fire department came. They're clearing out the old tree and blocking off the churro stand."

Nick nodded but didn't respond. Holly could see that he was

focusing on their mission.

Holly was struck by an idea. She texted Lucy back, instructing her to go to the school and get any of the ornaments left by the students. They were going to have to replace whatever broke in the storm.

Waiting for a response, Holly noticed the service bars on her device had disappeared.

"No service," she mumbled.

"That happens in some parts of Silverwood," Nick replied. "Some of these areas have no connection for a few miles. That's probably why no one builds out here."

Holly nodded and put her phone on her lap. It wouldn't do any good to stare at her screen. She just hoped they could find a good tree and get it back in time to start decorating.

Despite the snow tires on Nick's truck, it was a battle getting to the tree farm. Holly glanced into the side mirror to see if Eddie and Sean were keeping up. Judging from their headlights, they hit a few icy patches on the road, but they persevered and were not far behind.

She hadn't realized how tightly she'd been gripping the edge of her seat until Nick pulled to a stop at the side of the road by his tree farm. The trees were silhouettes in the distance, and Nick's shed of equipment stood, still and strong, like a soldier keeping watch over the land.

Nick turned to face her. His face seemed pale in the light of the dashboard. "You want to stay here out of the cold?"

"No way. I'm coming with you."

One corner of his mouth crept upward. "Okay. Let's get our

tree."

He shut off the engine and pushed his bomber hat down on his head. As he threw his door open, Eddie honked the car's horn to let them know they'd parked behind them.

The four of them held tightly to their hats and scarves as they trudged through knee-high snow toward the remaining full-grown trees on the lot. Icy snow hit Holly in the eyes and on her lips. She struggled to keep up with Nick, who walked ahead of her with a chainsaw in his grip. She wasn't sure if his long legs were helping him navigate his way, or if it was determination driving him forward. Whatever it was, she was feeling it. They were on a mission, and there was no turning back.

Misjudging her footsteps, Holly stumbled, throwing her arms out at her sides to keep her balance. It sounded as if a howl in the air was attacking her as the winds picked up and pushed her down. In an instant, strong arms were around her, lifting her up. For a moment neither Nick nor Holly could move for fear they'd be swept away with the storm. Holly couldn't even see where the other two men were, but she prayed they were holding their own. She could feel Nick's breath at her temple, but she couldn't see past his neck. Though the storm was screaming in her ears, she found comfort enveloped in Nick's arms.

At long last, the screaming stopped, dulling to a dull but constant moan. Holly risked lifting her head. Snow slapped her in the face, but the wind was less vicious.

Nick dipped his head. "Are you all right?"

"Yes." She swallowed hard and nodded. "Thank you."

"Should I bring you back to the truck?"

"No. Let's keep going."

"That was a close one," Eddie called from a few yards away. "You guys good?"

"Yeah," Nick answered, picking up his chainsaw from where he'd dropped it. "All clear."

"Sean?" Eddie called out.

Sean had been hunched over. As he stood up straight, he held up his glasses, one arm of which was bent. "Nothing major."

"Okay." Holly huffed a breath and nodded. "Let's find our tree."

Nick put his hand on Holly's back as they moved forward, one slow, strenuous step after the other.

After what seemed like forever, they came to a stop.

"What about this one?" Eddie's eyes were practically shut because of the blizzard. Still, the tree he pointed to was a fine specimen.

Holly looked up and took in the tall pine. It was about fifteen feet tall or so, from what she could tell, and mostly symmetrical. It was smaller than the tree from the festival, but it would have to do.

"Will it be hard to cut down?" Holly asked Nick.

"Depends on how much snow is in my face when I do it." Nick stomped closer to the tree and inspected it. "But I'm an experienced feller. I can handle it."

Holly stepped forward to help, but Cupid snatched the hem of her coat with his teeth and pulled her back when Nick's chainsaw started up. Somehow, she knew to listen to him. It could be dangerous, and, knowing nothing about felling a tree, she might just be in the way.

The three men managed to get the tree down in less time than she thought it would take. She followed with Cupid at her side as the tree was carried to a machine near Nick's shed on the property. It was a contraption with a large horizontal tube covered with netting. The tree was brought to the tube, top first, and pushed through. As it came out the other end, it was wrapped neatly and securely in the netting. This made it easier to carry, and Holly was able to help.

By the time they got back to Nick's truck. Holly was drenched with sweat. Nick lowered the back of the truck bed so the tree could be loaded. Tied down securely on the truck bed was Holly's sleigh. There was just enough room for the netted tree to fit beside it. Nick used rope to tie the tree down for their journey back to town.

"Looks like we're catching a break," Sean said, still breathing heavily with his hands on his sides. "Winds are dying down some more."

Holly hadn't even noticed because of how winded she'd been helping to lug the tree to the truck.

Eddie pointed to the car. "Let's head back. We'll meet you there."

Nick jumped down from the back of the truck. "We'll be right behind you."

Cupid was already at the truck's cab door, waiting to be let in.

Nick placed a hand on the small of Holly's back. "You're shivering. I'll get the heat going for you."

"I'm fine. I'm just glad we managed to find a tree. Let's get it back and win that contest for your father."

Nick placed his hands on Holly's upper arms. "You're amazing. You know that?"

"Me? I haven't done anything."

Still holding her, he rubbed her arms with his thumbs. Holly held her breath, wondering if he was going to kiss her. She shivered again. Cupid let out a bark. She couldn't tell what Nick was thinking, but he gave her a small smile before turning to open the passenger side door. After Cupid jumped in the cab, Nick helped Holly climb in.

As they maneuvered the truck to turn around and head back to town, Holly noticed that Eddie and Sean had already taken off ahead of them.

The drive back to town seemed less perilous. There were still slippery turns and steep slopes, which a truck Nick's size and weight was tricky to master. In front of them, the taillights of Sean and Eddie's car got smaller and smaller until they eventually disappeared from sight.

To keep herself calm, Holly pet Cupid, who was panting between her and Nick. They were almost there. There wasn't much farther to go. The heavy blizzard had diminished to light flurries, and the wind no longer howled in her ears.

We're going to make it, she said to herself.

Her breath hitched as the truck bounced on the road. Nick's grip on the wheel tightened as they drifted. Despite Nick's quick reaction, an unexpected patch of ice derailed their journey, and the front of the truck slid partway into a snowbank. Holly held Cupid back as the truck jolted to a stop.

"Hold on," Nick said, throwing the gears into reverse.

The tires were turning, kicking up snow, but the truck wouldn't budge. Nick tried a few more times but to no avail. With a tightened jaw, he threw the truck in park and shut off the engine. Glancing at Holly, he frowned and pulled out his phone.

"No signal," he said after checking his screen. He let out a grunt and scrubbed a hand down his face.

Holly checked her phone, just in case, but she had the same result.

Nick sighed and opened his door to get out and inspect the situation. Holly and Cupid joined him, finding him kicking snow away from one of the front tires.

"Any luck?" she asked.

"No." He chewed at his lip. "We're wedged on something. It'll need a tow."

When he stood and removed his bomber hat to swipe at his brow with his sleeve, Holly's heart broke for him. They were stuck and had no way to call for help. And she couldn't help but picture Mr. Mason's chance for treatment blowing away with the wind.

Chapter Twenty-Three

Holly looked toward the town and started walking.

"Holly, what are you doing?" Nick got hold of her wrist to stop her, obviously concerned.

"Maybe we can get a signal if we walk a little closer to town."

Nick studied her face. "Yeah, okay. I'll try up on the back of the truck. Maybe if I can get my phone high enough it will work. But, Holly, be careful."

"I will."

Cupid hopped over a hill of snow and followed Holly as she continued down the road with her phone held high in the air. As she took careful steps, she searched for a signal. There was no sign of any houses nearby, so finding a landline was an impossibility. Glancing over her shoulder sometime later, she realized she'd traveled rather far from the truck. She could barely make out Nick's arm as he held his phone up in the back of the truck, slowly pivoting his arm.

Making her way back to the truck, she could tell Nick must have been standing on the sleigh. With every step she took, her toes got more and more numb. Her teeth began chattering as the cold started to reach her bones. She carefully quickened her pace.

"Any luck?" she asked, a shiver shaking her shoulders.

"No. I'm hoping Sean and Eddie realize we're not behind them anymore and come back to help us.

Holly moved to the back of the truck, which Nick had lowered. She hoisted herself up to the truck bed and clenched her jaw to keep from shivering.

The tree was on the floor of the bed, secure in its net. She frowned. They were so close. They just needed to get the tree to town. She didn't want to quit their mission. Mr. Mason deserved more than that.

Holly realized she'd been leaning on the back of the sleigh. In the back of the sleigh was a pile of red tethers. Holly leaned into the sleigh and picked up some of the tethers to inspect them.

"Nick, are these the dog sled harnesses Rachel bought?"

Nick lowered his arm and turned to Holly. "Yeah. She put them in the sleigh so we could hook them up tomorrow evening."

Holly felt the wheels turning in her head. "How much weight can Alaskan Malamutes pull?"

"Well, it depends. A trained adult Malamute can pull around a thousand pounds. Some can even pull two thousand or more, depending on their build."

"That's amazing." Holly sized up the sleigh, hatching an idea. It took a moment for her to realize Nick was staring at her with a raised brow.

"What's going on in that head of yours?" he asked.

"Can you get the sleigh on the ground?"

He glanced at the sleigh and then his dolly. "Yeah." It sounded more like a question than a statement.

Holly made her way to the back of the truck. "Okay, good. Do it."

She could feel Nick watching her as she climbed down and crouched in front of Cupid. "All right, boy." Holly scratched behind his ears. "I need you to do your thing and call your brothers and sisters."

Nick leaned over the railing of the truck. "Holly, what are you doing?"

"Counting on a Christmas miracle." She stood and faced him, filled with a surge of optimism. "We're close enough to town that Cupid's siblings would hear him if he started howling, right?"

Nick's eyes widened. "Uh, yeah. I guess so."

"From what you've told me, they'll come running to him if he does. If you get the sleigh down, and we load the tree, we can hook up the dogs with Rachel's harnesses and get the tree back to the festival in time to decorate."

She clasped her hands together in front of her and waited for him to respond. His mouth opened, but he appeared as if he wasn't sure what to say.

"Nick, come on." Holly smiled at him. "You're the guy who's all about getting things done. And if nothing else, you made me realize I still love Christmas. Most importantly, we need to do this for your father. I don't think I could forgive myself if we didn't try everything we can think of to help him, long shot or not."

The smile returned to Nick's face. "Holly, did I ever tell you you're amazing?"

She smirked. "Once or twice."

He nodded. "Let's do this."

Holly turned back to Cupid, crouching down and sticking her chin in the air. She took a deep breath and then let out a long, "*Awoooooo!*"

Cupid tilted his head at her, as if trying to figure out what she was doing. He shifted his footing and whined. But by Holly's third howl, Cupid joined in. Together, they howled into the night sky, and Holly hoped their calls echoed all the way to Silverwood's town square. Holly hadn't seen all the dogs there, but she was willing to bet they were. If Nick's estimates were right about how much a Malamute could pull, and her estimate was right about how much weight the sleigh, the tree, Nick, and herself amounted to, then she would only need a couple more of the dogs to get them to town.

Mid-howl, she heard a thump behind her. She turned to see that Nick had successfully gotten the sleigh on the ground. When she stopped to listen, she heard a number of howls and barks answering Cupid's call.

"I think it's working." She said it quietly at first, but as the thrill of potential triumph coursed through her, she jumped up and shouted it. "I think it's working!"

She rushed to Nick and threw her arms around him. He laughed as he lifted her and twirled her around.

When he let her go, his eyes traveled over her face. "I can't believe it actually worked. Keep him howling so they can locate us. I'll load the tree and get the leads connected to the sleigh."

They followed through with their plan. Holly's voice was raw by the time an army of fur came into view. Not just two or three, but all eight siblings charged in their direction.

Holly had worked up such a sweat, the cold didn't bother her anymore. She was relieved and filled with adrenaline, and she couldn't remember being so elated.

The pack of dogs rushed to Cupid and began jumping around him. Cupid seemed happy to see them, rolling on his back in the snow and flailing his paws in the air at them

Nick handed Holly half of the leads. "Harness up the left team. I'll get the right."

Holly submerged herself into the pile of fluff, dodging wagging tails and canine kisses. She wasn't sure which dog was which or if she wasn't accidentally tangling the tethers, but she kept going until she had four dogs hooked up to the left row. At the head of the pack, Nick secured the lead harness on Rudolph, then pet his head. Rudolph panted and licked the red birthmark on his own nose.

Nick had the tree tied down in the sleigh, letting the back latch down to accommodate for the height. The top still stuck out of the sleigh, but it was netted, and Nick had been diligent fastening the ropes.

Holly and Nick looked over everything they had done. Holly was filled with enthusiasm. Warmth radiated through her body, and she couldn't help but bounce in place with elation. The dogs let out little impatient yips but stayed in place, waiting for their cue.

Nick extended a hand to Holly. "My lady, your chariot awaits."

She giggled as he helped her up into the sleigh. She sat on the cushioned bench, her skin tingling and her heart dancing in her chest. They were really doing it. They were going to save the day.

Nick took the reins and glanced at Holly. His eyes were sparkling as snow fell around them. "You ready to sleigh?"

Holly hooked her arm through his. "I could sleigh all day."

Chapter Twenty-Four

Silverwood's town square was all abuzz with how the nine dogs came charging back into town pulling Holly's glorious sleigh. Even as those who stayed helped set up the tree, it was all anyone could talk about. It had been like something out of a fairytale, and the fact that the dogs were named after Santa's reindeer made it all the more remarkable.

Lucy had come through with the ornaments, and Emily had even brought some from her personal collection. After Rachel cooled down the dogs from their arduous journey, she helped Eddie set up the sleigh on the red carpet with twinkling lights. Mr. Mason had already brought Avery home since it was past her bedtime. Holly was disappointed that Avery hadn't been able to see Dasher in action, but she was sure there was plenty of footage from everyone's phones. Besides, Avery would see the grand setup the next day during the competition.

It was just after midnight when the final decorations were placed on the tree. Just as he'd done before, Nick flipped the switch to light it up. This time, Holly was at his side. The small crowd that remained in the square applauded.

"It's beautiful," Holly said.

Nick took her hand and squeezed it. "It's because of you. You did this."

"We did this."

From the platform, Holly spotted Lucy waving at her.

Holly and Nick descended the stairs to approach Lucy and Sean. Lucy happily held up her Deluxe Megabox of Nick's cupcakes.

"I got what I came for," Lucy said.

"How did you get those?" Holly asked. "I thought the auction was stopped by the tree falling."

"It was." Lucy giggled. "But I made an offer, and they couldn't very well let the box go to waste, so here we are."

"Congratulations," Nick said.

"Lucy, aren't you exhausted?" Holly asked.

"You know, you'd think I would be, but I'm somehow filled with energy. Maybe it's a second wind."

"Thanks again for your help, Sean." Nick patted him on the shoulder.

"Of course." Sean nodded while squinting, because his glasses were broken. "Don't mention it."

"You really pulled it off." Lucy gazed at the tree. "It's spectacular. And the addition of that gorgeous sleigh—"

Lucy's eyes widened. Her grip on her cupcake box tightened as a gush of fluid dropped from between her legs onto the thin covering of snow.

Holly's jaw hung open. Lucy took a few steps back, gaping at the mess she'd just created.

"What?" Sean asked, squinting. "What happened?"

"My water broke." Lucy shook her head. "No. This can't happen now. I don't have my things. I need my bag with my focal point."

"Honey, calm down. I'll be your focal point."

"You can't even focus yourself."

"It'll be okay." Sean stepped forward to comfort her, but his foot slipped on the fluid on the ground. His leg slid out from under him, and he landed on his back with a *thud*.

"Sean!" Lucy bent slightly, but then she stopped and grabbed under her belly. Her brow creased and her jaw tightened. "Oh!"

Emily suddenly appeared at their sides. "Sean, are you all right? I saw you fall."

When Lucy moaned, Emily did a doubletake. "Oh my, are you in labor?"

Lucy cringed. "Maybe just a little?"

While Nick helped Sean to his feet, Holly hurried to Lucy's side, careful not to slip. "Okay, Lucy. I've got you."

Lucy latched on to Holly's hand. Her hold was so strong, it surprised Holly.

Sean winced and cupped the back of his head. "Ow."

"I'll call an ambulance." Nick took out his phone.

"No. I can drive." Emily pulled her car keys out of her coat pocket. "Let's get these two to my car."

Sean almost slipped again, but Nick caught him and propped him up.

"Here," Holly said to Lucy as they walked swiftly to Emily's car. "Let me hold that box for you."

"No way," Lucy said between moans. "This box is the only reason I left the house today. No one is taking it away from me."

"Okay, okay. It's yours." Holly glanced at Nick, who's eyes were wide.

"Sean?" Lucy looked over her shoulder.

"I'm here, honey," he answered, being led by Nick. "Wherever here is."

"We're almost at my car," Emily said.

Lucy let out a cry of pain, squeezing Holly's hand. Holly wanted to cry out but held it in for Lucy's sake.

Emily pushed the button on her fob to unlock the car. "Let's get them in. I can get them to the hospital in a few minutes."

Holly guided Lucy into the back seat, but Lucy wouldn't let go of her hand.

"Lucy."

"No, no, no. You have to come with me. I'm not letting go."

Holly glanced at Nick. "I … guess I'm going to the hospital?"

Nick nodded. "Yeah, of course. Get in with her. I'll put Sean in the front seat."

Holly swallowed hard. Lucy pulled her into the back seat with her.

Sean fumbled with his seatbelt, squinting at the contraption. Nick helped him and then shut the passenger side door.

"Okay, hold tight." Emily put the car in drive and took off.

Nick waved at Holly as they left, a concerned frown set on his face.

"I'll call you," Holly mouthed, hoping he understood.

"I'm not due for another week," Lucy whined.

"Well, mother nature does things on her own time," Emily told her. "Hold on. Tight curve coming up."

Holly felt as if she were being tossed around the back seat with her hand in a vise. "Lucy, maybe you can let go of my hand now? I won't leave you; I'm stuck in the car with you."

"No, please." Lucy blew out short, quick breaths. "This is helping."

"Could you at least switch to my left hand? This one's my painting hand."

"I can't let go. Don't make me."

"Then at least put down the cupcakes," Holly insisted.

Lucy shook her head. "Nuh-uh. My original focal point is at home in a bag. So now this box of cupcakes is my focal point. I need them."

Sean tried to look over his shoulder at Lucy, but not only was he wincing from his head injury, he couldn't seem to see Lucy clearly. "Are you all right, honey? Are you doing the breathing?"

Holly bit the inside of her lip to keep from shouting in pain. "Sean, you're looking at me. Lucy's directly behind you."

"Yes, yes," Lucy responded, sounding irritated. "I'm doing the breathing, but it still hurts. I think the birthing coach is a liar. Aahh!"

"We're almost there," Emily said calmly.

"Distract me, Holly," Lucy insisted, her voice whiney. "Tell me about my cupcakes."

"Well, uh, I can't see them, but I'm sure they're delicious. Um. Mine were."

Lucy squeezed her hand tighter. "Yeah, tell me more. Please!"

"Um, they were soft and fluffy. Just the right amount of sweet and spice. The first bite melted in my mouth like I was chewing on a cloud."

Lucy blew out a breath. "Mmm. Sounds perfect."

"Okay, we're here." Emily threw the car in park and hurried out of the car.

Sean opened his door but stumbled onto the concrete. Holly managed to get her door open and guided Lucy out of the car, box of cupcakes intact.

Emily was already racing to the car with a wheelchair.

"Perfect," Sean said, taking a seat in it.

"Sean!" Emily scolded. "It's for Lucy."

"Oh, right. Sorry." He felt around as he stood, making his way to the side of the wheelchair.

"Sit down," Holly told Lucy. She then took Sean's hand and placed it on one of the push bars. "We'll get you both inside."

Holly pushed the wheelchair to the hospital entrance. Lucy was cradling her cupcake box as if it was the baby. Sean nodded and said hello to a plant at the front doors.

Emily rushed ahead and spoke with the nurse at the front desk.

"Don't let them take my box away, Holly," Lucy said.

"I'm sure the doctors and nurses will make sure you have everything you need," Holly reassured her.

Two nurses greeted them. One took Sean to an examination room for his head injury, and the other brought Lucy to the labor ward.

"We'll just make sure your husband is all right," the nurse told Lucy, "and then we'll bring him to you."

Lucy held tight to her cupcake box. "Okay."

As she was wheeled away, she mouthed a "thank you" to Lucy and Emily.

They stood in the lobby for a moment, and Holly felt frazzled. "What do we do?" Holly asked.

"We could sit for a while." Emily gestured to the waiting area. "I'm sure we don't need to stay. It could take hours before the baby is born, but to tell you the truth I need to catch my breath."

"Same." Holly followed her to a couple of free chairs.

It was relatively quiet in the waiting room, with only a couple of people occupying the space in the middle of the night. The moment Holly sat down, she could feel the adrenaline zipping through her veins. She hadn't noticed before because of the ache in her hand. She shook her hand out. Luckily it didn't feel like Lucy had caused any injury, but she was in the right place if she had.

Holly placed a hand on Emily's arm. "So, with most of the excitement over, I finally have a chance to ask you if you had any more leads on someone taking over the school."

"No. But I'm not worried about it."

"Really? But what does that mean for your retirement?"

"I will figure it out. I'd love to keep it as my business but find someone to run it the way I want it run. None of these stencil-pushers. Someone who envisions the school the way I do. I'm not worried, though. If I've learned anything from tonight's events, it's that this town takes care of its own. I've seen what happens when people pull together, and I have faith in my people."

"Yeah, I've noticed that about Silverwood." Holly sighed. "It's a miraculous place."

"Have you given any more thought about whether you're staying or going back to New York?"

Holly smirked. "I have to say, I've been given a lot to think about. But the reasons for staying are pretty much outweighing the reasons for going."

"Reasons like Nick?"

"Among others. But, yeah. I can't deny that on the list of reasons to stay in Silverwood, Nick's at the top."

Chapter Twenty-Five

Holly opened her eyes, stretching in her bed. The last thing she remembered was texting Nick to let him know she was home. Lucy had still been in labor when Holly and Emily left the hospital, but they'd both agreed it would serve everyone better if they went home and got some sleep. Especially after such an adventurous night. She was surprised she'd actually made it to her bed before passing out.

Picking up her phone to check the time, she realized she'd slept almost until noon. She also realized there was a message on her phone from Lucy. She sat up straight in the bed, her heart pumping as she read the message.

> Holly! She's here! I had the baby at 4:10 in the morning. Ugh, I haven't stayed up that late since my party girl days. Anyway, I wanted to say thank you for everything. We can't wait for you to meet our Samantha Grace. Sean and I are already so in love with her. PS – the cupcakes were amazing!

Holly laughed at the last sentence and put down her phone. She was filled with joy. Not only for Lucy and Sean, but for herself. She felt good. She felt content. She felt …

Inspired.

Holly jumped out of bed and rushed to the living room to dig into her art supplies. She was invigorated as she set up a canvas and primed it. Her mind was filled with colors and light. With visions of the events that carried out during the last twenty-four hours. With the way that Nick made her feel.

When her phone buzzed sometime later, she realized she'd been painting for three hours. A small sense of panic filled her seeing Nick's name on her screen.

She hadn't missed the judging, had she? She couldn't have. It was still light outside.

"Hello?"

"Holly. Hi!"

"Hi, Nick. Am I late?"

"No, not at all. But I've got a very energetic eight-year-old here asking for you. She insists on hearing your version of last night's adventure."

Holly smiled. "Of course. I'd be happy to accommodate. I just have to wash a layer of paint off my skin and then visit the newest little citizen of Silverwood at the hospital first."

"Lucy had her baby!"

"Yes. A girl. Samantha Grace."

"I take it everyone is fine and healthy."

"Lucy says they're in love, so I guess so."

The line was quiet for a moment. Holly wondered if they'd

been disconnected.

"That's great," he finally said. "I'm so happy for them."

A thought struck her. She wondered if Nick was envious of the family Lucy and Sean had created. Of the family his sister had.

"Me too," Holly said. "Tell Avery I'll be there soon."

She arrived at the town square while the sun was still up. Christmas music was playing through the street speakers, and Holly found herself humming along. When she walked by The Gingerbread House, she spotted Cupid and Dasher sleeping on the floor inside.

Totally relatable, she thought to herself.

"Holly!" Avery came running at her from the town square, throwing her arms around her waist in a hug when she reached her. "I've been waiting for you for hours!"

"Sorry about that." Holly opened her phone and showed her a picture of Lucy's baby. "I had to make a pitstop to visit this little girl."

"Is that Lucy's baby?"

"Yep."

"She's so cute! Is she bringing her to class?"

Holly laughed. "Probably not right away."

Nick and Mr. Mason approached them. Mr. Mason wore a Santa suit but hadn't put on the hat yet.

"Well, hello, Santa," Holly said. "You look awesome."

"I was about to say the same thing to you." Mr. Mason rubbed his beard. "There's something different. It's like you're glowing."

Holly laughed. "I think it's just Christmas getting to me." Her eyes met with Nick's. "How are you holding up?"

"I'm doing all right if I don't stop to think about how important this contest is."

Mr. Mason clapped his son on the back. "Stop worrying, Nicky. It serves no purpose."

"Nick," one of the workers—Darby, Holly remembered—called from the shop door. "There's some papers Rachel said you need to fill out before the judges get here."

"Oh, right." Nick placed a hand on Holly's back. "I'll be back in a bit."

"Sure. No rush."

Mr. Mason stepped closer to Holly. He looked as if he had tears in his eyes. "Holly, I really want to thank you."

"Don't thank me yet. We need to win first."

He took her hand in both of his. "No, really. Even if we don't win, what you did, what you managed to pull off … it was incredible. And it means so much to me that you cared enough to see it through."

She couldn't hold back. She put her arms around him and squeezed, fighting off the onset of tears. "I hope it works," she whispered.

"Me too."

"Holly?" Avery tugged on her coat.

Holly released Mr. Mason and faced Avery with a smile. "Yeah?"

"I also want to thank you," she said. "Mom let me open one

present early, and I picked yours. I love the art supplies. I can't wait to make you something."

"You're welcome. I'm sure I'll love whatever you create."

Avery hugged her once more.

"All right," Nick said as he emerged from the shop. "Stop hogging the town hero. Give the rest of us a chance."

Rachel stood in the doorway of the shop. "Daddy needs you inside anyway. He won't tell me what it's about, though, so you'll have to ask him yourself."

"Ooh, sounds like a top-secret mission." Mr. Mason winked at her. "I better come too."

Holly laughed. "Don't worry, Avery. We'll catch up in a bit so I can tell you all about how courageous the dogs were last night."

Avery jumped up and clapped her hands. "Yes! I can't wait!"

They disappeared inside the shop, leaving Holly and Nick alone.

"So, you saw Lucy's baby?" Nick closed the distance between them and reached for her fingers. He intertwined them with his, keeping his gaze on her face.

"Yeah. She looks like an angel. And Lucy seems fine, too. Kept asking the nurse to bring her more Jell-O."

Nick laughed. "Sounds like Lucy."

Holly let out a slow breath. "Take me to see the tree."

"It would be my pleasure."

They walked hand in hand to the center of the town square. Now, in the light of the setting sun, Holly could fully appreciate the beauty of the tree. It was breathtaking, and the sleigh full of wrapped gifts standing beside it, sitting comfy on the red carpet with a dusting of snow, made the picturesque image complete. Holly thought about her dad and how he would be pleased that it was used for this purpose. She could almost imagine him smiling down on the scene and wishing them luck.

Holly smirked. "Not bad for a bunch of dazed folks working in the dark in the middle of a snowstorm, right?"

"Pretty amazing, actually."

"The judges are going to be blown away."

Nick smiled but averted his gaze. "Listen, before they get here, there's something I want to give you."

A wide grin spread across Holly's face. She tucked a strand of hair behind her ear. "Okay."

Nick slipped a small box out of his coat pocket. It was wrapped in shiny red paper and secured with a white, silk bow.

Holly's heart sped up as she took it from him.

"Go ahead and open it," he whispered.

Feeling like a little kid, she undid the bow and ripped the paper away. Lifting the lid from the box inside, she found a silver necklace with a crystal snowflake pendant. It glistened in the twilight.

"Nick, it's gorgeous."

He took the necklace out and undid the clasp. "It's to commemorate the mission we went on last night and to celebrate the fact that we pulled it off."

He moved behind her, and she lifted her hair away from her shoulders. A chill traveled up her spine as Nick's hands brushed against her neck. He closed the clasp and let go of the necklace.

Moving back to face her, he gazed at the necklace and nodded.

"Suits you."

She ran her fingertips over the crystal snowflake. "I love it. Thank you. I have something for you, too, but it's not ready. So, you'll have to wait."

He took her hands in his. "I can wait for you forever, as long as I know you're coming."

"Nick! Holly! They're here." Mr. Mason came rushing toward them with his Santa hat in his hands. "Rachel, Eddie, and Avery are bringing the dogs. And the judges are waiting for you to escort them to the tree."

"Did Viola get them all hot chocolates?" Nick asked.

"With extra whipped cream." Mr. Mason winked and placed the Santa hat on his head.

Nick squeezed Holly's hands before releasing them. "Here we go."

"You've got this," Holly told him. "We're going to win."

Nick nodded, visibly swallowing, and went to meet the judges.

Mr. Mason put a hand on Holly's shoulder. "I better take my place on the sleigh. Any Christmas wishes you'd like to tell Santa? Now's your chance."

"Aside from Silverwood winning this contest, I feel like all my wishes came true. Even the ones I didn't know I wanted."

Mr. Mason chuckled, his hands on his belly as it jiggled. Then he turned and climbed onto the sled.

"Holly!"

Holly turned to find Emily coming toward her. "Hi, Emily."

"Lucy's baby is beautiful, isn't she?"

"Yes. I was just telling Nick that she looks like an angel."

Emily smiled. "So, listen. I have a proposition for you."

Holly's brow furrowed. "You do?"

"I know you've been trying to figure out what you want to do and if you're going back to New York or maybe sticking around here for a while. I thought I'd give you something to consider if you're leaning toward staying in Silverwood."

"Okay. What is it?"

"I'd like you to manage the school."

Holly could only blink for a moment. "Me? Really?"

"Yes. I know you have the school's best interest at heart. And I know what lengths you're willing to go to for a worthy cause. That's exactly what I need in someone to take over the school. Not to mention I really want the school in the hands of an artist. It would still by mine, but I'd be more like the silent corporate head who just signs the checks."

Holly gently bit her lip. She felt a floating sensation, like someone or something was lifting her up and taking her away from her burdens.

"Emily, this is an amazing offer." Holly wrung her hands. "Can I think about it?"

"Yes, of course." Emily smiled and patted her on the shoulder. "I wanted to let you know you have options."

"I really appreciate it, Emily. Thank you."

Emily looked past Holly's shoulder. "Looks like the cavalry has arrived."

Holly turned to see Rachel, Eddie, and Avery leading the nine Alaskan Malamutes to the sleigh. Holly and Emily made room as the dogs were hooked up to the harnesses. Once the dogs were in place, Avery climbed up in the sleigh next to her grandfather. She waved at Holly, beaming.

"That's quite incredible," one of the judges was saying to Nick as they approached. "And their real names are Dasher and Dancer and Prancer ... and so on?"

"They truly are," Nick replied.

"Even if they weren't," another judge said, "how amazing is it that Rudolph actually has a red nose?"

The judges laughed. Mr. Mason let out a couple *ho ho ho*s for good measure, waving to the judges. He shook the reins, which were adorned with bells that rang, adding a little more magic to the scene.

"It's not the biggest tree," another judge said, writing something on his notepad. "But it is beautifully decorated. And the package as a whole is more impressive than anything else we've seen."

"This was our last stop on the circuit," the first judge said to Nick. "If you give us some time to deliberate, we can actually reach a decision tonight and let you know. In, say, half an hour?"

The judges checked with each other, each of them nodding in response.

"Yes, of course." Nick let out nervous laughter. "Feel free to use a table at The Gingerbread House. Or anywhere you'd like, actually. And take all the time you need."

The judges nodded and thanked Nick, taking one last look at the tree, sleigh, and dogs before returning in the direction of The Gingerbread House.

Nick's shoulders sagged once they were out of sight. Holly

hurried to his side.

"They love it," she told him.

"Are you sure? I couldn't tell. And I don't know what our competition has done."

"Stop worrying." She took his hand. "We've got this."

Mr. Mason, who'd stepped off the sleigh, patted Nick on his back. "And if not, there's always next year."

"Exactly," Holly said. "We'll blow their Christmas stockings off next year if we have to."

Nick cocked a brow. "Next year? You'll be in Silverwood for next year's contest? You'll come back?"

"Or … maybe I just won't leave."

A smile spread on Nick's face. "Really?"

She smiled and shrugged. "Anything's possible."

Nick grabbed her hands. "Did my plan actually work?"

Holly laughed. "Don't get ahead of yourself. Let me make up my mind in good time."

"Yes, of course." He squeezed her hands. "Take all the time you need. No pressure."

"How about we wait to see how this turns out first." She leaned in closer to Nick. "He puts up a good front, but I'm sure your father is beside himself right now."

Nick glanced at his father. "Yeah. I'll, uh, try to distract him."

The half hour of waiting for the judges to make their decision seemed to have dragged on, but Holly knew it was only in their heads. She rubbed at her arms, the cold taunting her as they waited. Nick had resorted to biting his nails, which got him a light slap on the back of his head from his sister. Mr. Mason was quiet and reserved, keeping to himself on the bench of the sleigh.

At long last the judges emerged from The Gingerbread House. Nick stood up, fidgeting with his coat buttons as they approached. Holly felt as if she couldn't breathe until they announced their decision.

"Mr. Mason," the first judge said to Nick, "I'm happy to announce that we have decided to declare Silverwood as this year's Christmas Tree Decorating Contest winner."

The Masons shouted with excitement and glee, jumping up and embracing each other. Nick pulled Holly into their group hug and kissed her on the head. Everyone within hearing distance cheered for them as well.

"We will make an official press release tonight," said the judge, "but here's your certificate. We'll transfer the cash prize to the account you've noted in your paperwork next week. Congratulations."

Nick took the certificate and hugged the judge. "Thank you so much!"

Rachel shook their hands. "Thank you. Thank you so much."

The crowd was still celebrating as the judges left the town square. The music seemed louder and people were dancing in the street.

Holly approached Mr. Mason, who had tears running down his cheeks. They'd done it. Mr. Mason would be able to afford his medication for many, many years. "I'm so happy for you," she said. "Congratulations."

"I'm at a loss for words." Mr. Mason wiped the tears from his face, smiling at her. "This is the merriest Christmas I could ever imagine."

Holly glanced at Nick. "I have to agree with you there, Mr. Mason."

Nick caught her looking at him and rushed to her, sliding his hands to her waist. His eyes darted over her face before leaning in and kissing her.

Epilogue

H olly swiped her forehead with her arm. "All right. That's all for today. Make sure you clear your stations."

It had been a busy week. There was more to learning to manage the school than she had thought, but she was absolutely loving it. Emily promised her she'd stay to train her until Holly felt comfortable enough to take the reins on her own. She had to admit, it was a challenge that kept her motivated. And she loved seeing the art the children were creating.

Every day, the children brought an energy with them that was so pure and unfiltered, so full of promise. Holly thrived as she took in their passion for art, in turn escalating the passion for her own art. She no longer felt held down by big time business standards when she painted. She painted because she loved it, not because she wanted to sell something or had to pay the rent.

And she felt like she was serving a purpose, giving back to the community by supporting young artists-to-be and encouraging them to express themselves the way they wanted to.

The kids left the building, waving goodbye to her. As the last student went through the door, someone else came in. Holly smiled as Nick entered the lobby, looking handsome in his plaid winter coat. He removed his wool bomber hat and smirked at her, and Holly practically swooned at the sight of his dimple.

"Nick Mason," she said.

"Holly St. Ives."

She hadn't seen him all week because of how busy she'd been, but it was Friday, and they had plans to spend the weekend together.

"Sorry about the mess," she said, moving some paperwork on the front counter.

"The view seems perfect to me."

She caught a glimpse of her reflection in the glass of her office's window. Her hair was clumped on her head in a messy bun, and she had paint splotches on her face.

She let out a small laugh. "You look pretty good too. I'll be ready in a minute."

He followed her as she unlocked her office and went inside. She used wet wipes to get the paint off her face and slipped the hairband from her bun. Her hair cascaded down to her shoulders in waves, but she was sure she'd need to run a brush through it.

"How's your dad?" she asked.

"He's doing well." Nick leaned against the door frame. "He should be set with his medication for a long time coming."

"That's great. I'm so happy it all worked out." She grabbed her purse. "I just have to kill the lights and lock up."

"Okay. I've got something in my car I want to show you."

"Oh yeah? What is it?"

He snickered. "Just finish up so you can see for yourself."

"You know," she said as she started switching off lights in the school, "I sometimes feel like the whole tree rescue thing was a dream. Like, did we really do that? Would anyone really believe that we got nine Alaskan Malamutes to come rescue us in the mountains and pull us back in a sleigh? I mean, when I told my mom what had happened, she thought I was making it up."

"Christmas miracles," Nick said. "Things sometimes happen the way they're supposed to whether people believe it or not."

"Hmm." She narrowed her eyes at him. "Are you talking about me staying in Silverwood?"

"Something like that. Okay, let's go."

She shut the last light off and they stepped outside. After she locked the front door, she followed Nick to his car.

"What did you want to show me?" she asked.

"Well, the painting you gave me was such a great gift that I felt I needed to do more for you."

Holly scoffed. "What? No. You gave me a beautiful necklace."

"I know. But I wanted to give you something you needed."

"Oh. All right."

He opened the back of his car, and Holly peered inside. Lying in the truck was a painted wooden mailbox carved into the shape of a sleigh. The side of the sleigh read *St. Ives*.

"You made this?" she asked, running her hand over the wood.

"Yep. I was sick of looking at that busted old mailbox in front of your house," he joked. "I'll set it up for you."

She leaned up and pecked him on the lips. "That's so sweet of you. Thank you."

"I just figured, if you're really staying in Silverwood, then this kind of seals you in."

"Oh, so this is a contract?" she joked.

"Something like that." He winked at her and went to the passenger side of the door, opening it for her. "But seriously. No regrets?"

She ran a hand over his cheek. "None whatsoever."

"Just the two words I wanted to hear you say."

Holly let out a laugh. "What do you say we get some dinner?"

"I'm in."

"Hey, how's Avery. Is she coming back to class next week?" They were still standing outside the car, with Holly leaning her back against it.

"Yes, she can't wait. She just needed to fight off this cold, but she's such a trooper, she's already feeling better."

"I'm glad. I'm really quite fond of her. Of your whole family, actually. They're so lovely. I kind of feel like they've become mine."

Nick elbowed her. "Maybe they will be. One day."

Holly bit her cheek. "Don't get ahead of yourself, Nicky."

"All kidding aside," he said, leaning closer to her, "I'm glad you like them. They like you too."

"I love how you take care of them."

"Are you saying I have a hero complex? Because you might want to take a look in the mirror."

"I think I'd rather look at you."

He smiled and took her hand. Holly couldn't help but sigh. All the pieces to this puzzle she had been trying to figure out suddenly fit. This man had become a part of her heart—a big part. And she couldn't imagine living her life without him. And Silverwood …

She felt like deep down it had been her home all along.

"It's funny," she said, intertwining her fingers with his. "I know he's not named after the mythical god of love and attraction, but ultimately, it was Cupid who brought us together. It's like he knew we were meant for each other."

Nick nodded. "I have a feeling he's smarter than the rest of us."

"I think you're right."

He pulled her into his arms and dipped his head. She smiled as his lips brushed against hers, and then she closed her eyes and let him kiss her, fully, deeply, and completely.

Acknowledgements

Though I've always wanted to write romance, I never had the nerve to dive into it until my amazing agent, Italia Gandolfo, pitched me the opportunity. I've been writing stories with elements of magic, mostly, so Christmas in Silverwood was entirely out of my wheelhouse. But I'm so glad I didn't run away from the chance to tell Holly and Nick's story. I'm so grateful for everything Italia has done to nurture my writing career. I truly am blessed.

I'm so honored to be part of the Vesuvian team, and I thank everyone involved for their encouragement and support.

As always, I have to thank everyone who has stuck around to support me: my friends, colleagues, and especially my family. A special thanks goes out to Viola Kretzschel for letting me use her name in the story. You're a star!

And of course I need to thank my two lovely pups, Kovu and Kascha, for inspiring me to include lovable canines in a story about love and miracles.

About the Author

 Dorothy Dreyer is an award-winning, *USA Today* bestselling author. Born in Angeles City, Philippines to a Filipino mother and American Father, Dorothy grew up a military brat, living in Guam, Massachusetts, South Dakota, New Jersey, and New York. Dorothy is bilingual, speaking fluent English and German, and teaches English to children at a multilingual school in Frankfurt, Germany, where she resides with her family and two Siberian huskies. She always has a story or two running through her brain, and she loves to share those stories with anyone willing to listen.

www.DorothyDreyer.com